GARY CHURCH

WHEN JUSTICE IS DONE

JOHNNY BLACK
MAN AND LEGEND 1874

This book is a work of fiction. The characters, locales, places, names and incidents are all a creation of the author's imagination or used in a fictitious manner. Any resemblance to real persons, living or dead or to actual events is completely coincidental.

ISBN: 9781661356170

When justice is done,
it brings joy to the righteous
but terror to evildoers.
Proverbs 21:15

Dedicated to the Beacham clan.

Good people.

PROLOGUE

Johnny Black was lying in bed, awake. When Red, the rooster, announced the dawn, Johnny rolled out. He was careful not to disturb his wife, Rosalinda or his daughter, Lucrecia, who had recently turned two and was asleep in her own small bed. He arose to a very cold home, this mid-November morning, 1874, but Johnny didn't mind. Pulling on his trousers and boots, then putting on his shirt, he went into the kitchen and started a fire in the cookstove. He filled the coffeepot and set it on the stove before heading out to the barn to feed the horses and have his morning discussion with Henry Bear; the man who oversaw the combination farm, horse and cattle ranch. Johnny had started out breeding horses, but had added longhorns, expanded his corn and wheat fields and planted a number of acres in produce.

When Rosalinda arose, twenty minutes later, the warmth was already spreading through the house. Lucrecia continued to sleep soundly, snuggled in her blankets. By the time Rosalinda had begun the preparations for breakfast, she found the morning's milk and eggs on the back porch; placed there by Henry Bear who insisted on performing these chores himself as he had done most mornings since he came to the Black homestead. Henry had been a slave for much of his life, but now lived on the Black ranch in his own home, which he shared with Venus, a pretty black woman, whom he had married just over two years before. Born into slavery, Henry didn't know his surname, but folks had always told him he was big as a bear, so he had taken the name Bear.

As Johnny walked out to the barn, he cast an eye over the dozen mares in the corral. All the horses were in their eighth or ninth month of pregnancy. Another half dozen mares, also late in their gestation periods, were in the barn. The mares were being monitored as they should foal eleven months after conception if all went well. A second corral held Rosalinda's horse, Patience, and Henry's horse, Spartacus. He didn't see his own horse, Loco, a Percheron, who stood some nineteen hands tall and refusing to be penned up, roamed freely about the place. As he neared the barn, Johnny was pounced on by his three dogs, Flop, Perro and Princesa, all jumping and licking at him in greeting. Johnny stopped to rub and talk to them, their greetings always warming his heart.

"Good morning boss," said Henry Bear, as Johnny entered the barn.

Henry's voice had come from the feed locker, where, by the light of a lantern, he was filling a pail with oats and beans for the horses.

"Good morning Henry," responded Johnny, as he climbed a ladder to the loft which held hay. As he stepped up into the loft, he saw two sets of cat eyes peering at him from the darkness. The two cats had adopted Henry Bear and the three had lived in the barn until Henry finished his house and moved into it with his new wife, Venus. He had invited the cats to move with him, and they visited from time to time, but they always returned to the barn.

Johnny found the pitchfork and was soon tossing hay out into the corrals and down the trap door to the barn floor where Henry moved it into the mare's feeding troughs in the stalls. Loco appeared and Henry tossed some hay out to him before taking him a bucket of oats and beans.

The early feeding complete, Johnny and Henry stepped outside and Johnny lit one of the small cigarillos he favored and Henry loaded his pipe. For a few minutes, they stood in the cold morning, smoking in silence.

"How are the young men doing?" asked Johnny, referring to two young black boys Henry had hired to help on a part-time basis with the farming and produce operations.

"They're doing well," said Henry, smiling. "You still thinking to take on somebody, to manage the horses and beeves?"

"Yes, I put word out that I need a hand. I reckon somebody will show up soon. I'll be good so long as I get some help by the Spring. You're doing a fine job with the farming and the produce, Henry, so I don't give that any thought."

The two finished their smokes and with a nod, Johnny and Henry, as one, turned and headed to their respective homes for breakfast.

CHAPTER 1

Rosalinda smiled as Johnny stepped into the kitchen, the cold air following him in. The two kissed and as Rosalinda set the table, Johnny poured himself some coffee. After the breakfast dishes were cleared, Johnny and Rosalinda enjoyed a cup of coffee together as they did most mornings.

"Johnny, I have a small list of things I need; some of it for Thanksgiving, just next Thursday. You do remember we're expected at my parents? Why don't you go to San Antonio tomorrow night and play poker and Saturday you could stop by the general store?"

Johnny smiled as he sipped his coffee. He knew that she knew full well he could easily go in to town on Saturday and return without a problem. Rosalinda knew he liked to play cards from time to time and was often ahead of his own feelings. Now that he thought about it, he would surely enjoy playing and catching up with the regular players.

"Well, it'd put me off my schedule, but if you need something I can rearrange some things, talk to Henry Bear…"

Johnny lifted his cup to his mouth and peered at Rosalinda over it.

She stared at him with her 'I see right through you look', but smiled and said, "Thank you my husband."

Johnny laughed and Rosalinda joined in.

The next day, the noon meal finished, Rosalinda handed Johnny her list., and said, "Oh Johnny, do you recall Mrs. Madison, the elderly woman that quilts with our group?"

"I think so. They farm a little and raise hogs, as I recall."

"Yes. The thread on the list is for her. I mentioned you were going to town and she asked if you would pick some up. Would it be too much trouble to drop it by her place on your way home? She wrote down directions."

"Sure," said Johnny, thinking that the quilting meeting was last Tuesday, so Rosalinda had been thinking this out. Bless her, he was looking forward to the poker game.

The following afternoon, the weather still cold, Johnny saddled Loco, talked to the dogs, had a word with Henry and after stopping at the house to kiss Rosalinda and Lucrecia, mounted up and rode for San Antonio.

Johnny checked into the Menger hotel in San Antonio Friday afternoon, had supper at Jose's, one of his favorite restaurants and then sauntered down to the Gentleman's Saloon to join the poker game. The regulars were surprised and happy to see him. The men discussed prices, politics and the ups and downs in their own personal worlds. As was his custom, Johnny listened, commented and smiled, but didn't add much, however, he enjoyed the camaraderie and card game.

Saturday morning, after fulfilling the shopping list at the general store, he headed for the Madison place to drop off the thread for Mrs. Madison. The morning was clear, but cold as Johnny and Loco made their way out of San Antonio and into Medina County.

CHAPTER 2

"Whoa, boy," said Johnny Black, as he fished a paper with directions written on it out of his greatcoat pocket and studied them.

The November wind had picked up making it feel even colder. He had only skimmed the directions earlier, sure he would find his way easy enough, but he had come to a split in the road and wasn't sure which way to continue. He read the directions carefully this time.

At the end of the page he read: *A half-mile after the road splits you'll see our house, it has a small flower garden surrounded by a low rock wall beside the porch.*

Johnny fished a cigarillo and a match from his pocket and lit up. As he smoked he looked around. It was so typical of people giving directions, he thought. They knew the way so well, they often overlooked important details. In this case, Mrs. Madison had failed to indicate which way to proceed when the road split.

He smiled to himself. It wasn't a large concern. At most, if he traveled a half-mile and found he had taken the wrong road, he wouldn't have wasted much time. The road he was on seemed to veer left, while the other one went right. It was likely he was meant to stay to the left, he decided, clucking a little and shaking the reins to alert Loco to his desire to start again.

He was good at judging distance and he found a house at what he perceived was a half-mile down the road, however, it had no rock wall and no flower garden. In fact, the place was in disrepair and not well-kept, although smoke rose from a limestone smokestack. Johnny sighed. He had in fact, gone the wrong way and he was about to turn back when, as was his habit, he scanned the area and not far from the house he saw a corral with a lone horse standing in it. Johnny sat Loco and studied the horse. It was a good hundred and fifty yards away, but he could see the animal wasn't right. It's ribs and shoulder bones protruded. It must be sick, thought Johnny. Without even thinking, he nudged Loco into action, walking him out to the corral which held the horse.

The corral was attached to a barn that needed repair. Johnny dismounted and climbing up on the corral fence, dropped to the other side and approached the horse as he talked quietly to him. The corral was barren except for a water trough, half full of water. Reaching the horse, Johnny stroked his neck and began to examine him. In a minute he knew the problem. The horse was starving.

Entering the barn, lit by spaces where boards were missing, Johnny was surprised to find another horse, this one healthy. He also found a supply of oats and hay. Filling a pail with oats, Johnny took it out to the horse in the corral and after returning to the barn, he carried an armload of hay out to the animal.

As the horse ate, Johnny talked quietly to it and stroked its neck. The horse turned its head and nuzzled Johnny's hand.

Suddenly a voice cracked through the cold, still morning air, "What the hell do you think you're doing!"

Turning his head to seek out the source of the voice, Johnny saw a large man, his whisker-stubbled face red with rage, standing just outside the corral, holding a scattergun at waist level, its barrel pointing toward Johnny.

"Good morning," said Johnny, calmly, but without feeling. "I was looking for the Madison place, saw this horse and thought it was abandoned."

"Well it ain't as you can see, so get out of my corral and off my property before I blow a hole through you!"

After giving the horse's neck one last stroke, Johnny nodded and, to the surprise of the man with the shotgun, walked toward the man rather than away from him. The man, without thinking, stepped back as Johnny reached the corral fence and climbed over, jumping down just feet from where the big man, with a look of surprise on his face, stood.

"I think your horse is starving," said Johnny, as though the two men were discussing the weather.

His grin exposing broken, rotting teeth, the man said, "You're right about that. The dumb animal kicked me. I aim to teach him a lesson."

Johnny nodded his understanding. "Tell you what, I'll buy him from you," said Johnny.

"He ain't for sale," replied the man.

"I'll give you double his value," Johnny responded.

The man's eyes squinted as he studied Johnny. "Well, that's an odd offer. How much we talking?"

"If that horse was healthy, he might bring a hundred dollars, but he's not."

The big man scowled. "That's a two-hundred-dollar horse and double that would be four hundred dollars."

"I'll give you a hundred dollars," replied Johnny. "That's double his current worth."

The man studied Johnny, looked over at the starving horse and decided to accept before Johnny could change his mind.

"You're robbing me, but okay."

"I have the money. Can you write?"

"I can write my name and read a little."

"I'll write a bill of sale for you to sign and I'll pay you. But first I'm going to teach you not to starve animals," replied Johnny, lifting his hat from his head and turning to place it on top of a corral post.

This statement brought a huge smile to the man's face. "I was just looking for an excuse to bash your head in," said the man. "Teach you to mind your own business."

As he finished his statement and Johnny turned toward him, the man, who had switched his hands to the end of the shotgun while Johnny's head was turned, swung the gun at Johnny's head with all the force he could muster.

Johnny did two things simultaneously. He ducked and stepped into the man. The big man had three inches and ninety pounds on Johnny, but as the man's arms swung to his left with the force of the long weapon, Johnny's right hand arced up and over in a looping overhand right that made contact with the man's face, right between his eyes.

Without hesitation, Johnny pivoted on the balls of his feet, bringing a left hook from below his belt, striking the man with enormous power on the left side of his head. Stepping back, Johnny began to pummel the man's face with left jabs. He hit him again and again, Johnny's face contorted with rage at the thought of the starving horse.

Johnny was so focused he didn't see the second man who had come from the back of the house. Seeing the fight, the man circled around and picked up a piece of broken post. Stepping behind Johnny, he lifted it to hit Johnny in the back of the head with it.

The injury to Johnny would likely have been serious, maybe deadly, but something initiated a response in Loco. Perhaps the man holding the broken post triggered a memory. Or maybe it was the threat to Johnny, but as the man crept up behind Johnny, Loco, his neck extended, his teeth bared, his eyes wild, charged the man with the post and clamped his teeth on the man's upper shoulder. As his teeth clamped down, Loco's momentum kept him moving, the man was dragged, screaming, for ten yards before Loco released him.

Loco was just a blur as he went by, but the man's screams caused Johnny to step back and look for the source. He saw Loco stop and whirl, and then he noticed the man on the ground. Turning his attention back to the man he was fighting he quickly leaned hard to his left to avoid a right roundhouse swing meant to render Johnny unconscious.

The right-handed blow missing, the big man stumbled as Johnny stepped back and looked around. He saw the man Loco had bitten rolling on the ground, holding his shoulder and moaning. The broken post lying a few yards away. Loco standing, watching. The starving horse still eating.

His hot rage now turning to cold resolve, once again Johnny stepped close to the big man and began to methodically hammer his face and body with blows from both hands.

Finally, his face a bloody mess, the man said, "I quit."

Leaning in close to the man, Johnny hissed, "I'll be checking on you from time to time and may the Lord have mercy on you if I ever think you're mistreating any animal again."

After Johnny had written out the bill of sale, the man signed it and Johnny paid him with a final warning. Johnny, rope in hand, climbed into the corral. The horse, his ears forward, his nostrils relaxed, walked up to Johnny and pushed his head into Johnny's shoulder.

Early that afternoon, Johnny, the starving horse trailing on the rope, the bill of sale in his pocket, rode up to the barn on his homestead and dismounted. Rosalinda, seeing him arrive, put coffee water on the stove to heat and went to her room to brush her hair.

Turning the horses over to the two boys who helped on the place, to be brushed and fed, Johnny told them, "Give the new horse an extra ration each time you feed him," then he walked down to the house where Rosalinda greeted him with a fresh cup of coffee and a smile.

"I see we have a new horse," she said. "Did it follow you home?"

"Sort of," said Johnny.

"Johnny Black. You and animals," said Rosalinda.

CHAPTER 3

The American Civil War broke out in April 1861, and Caleb, an eighteen-year-old farm boy in Ohio, gave it only the briefest consideration. Although he had been educated at his parent's insistence, he gave politics and the government little thought. His days were long, beginning before the sun rose and ending at dark. The work was physically demanding and his thoughts were filled with the girl that lived down the way.

However, as the war expanded and the states began to raise armies, Caleb became caught up in the excitement and he considered joining the army. The lure of adventure had been strong, but his parents needed his help on the farm and he had fallen deeply in love with the neighbor girl and thought of little else.

As the war continued, he took more of an interest in it as their neighbors lost sons and relatives and men began to return physically impaired. But his life's path was set and he was content. The war had raged for almost two years when Caleb, twenty years of age and a month shy of his wedding date, received a draft notice, and he accepted it without question. If he had already been married, it was likely he would never have been forced into the war, as single men had to be called before married men could be pressed into service. Others, with means, were paying substitutes to take their places, or men had the option of paying three hundred dollars, but he had neither the money nor the heart to do so. This was his fate and he accepted it. His fiancée wanted to marry before he left, but his fear of leaving a new wife a widow, made him put it off until his return.

In the early days of his service, he had been wounded twice, but recovered, then he was badly wounded in March of '65 and was still healing when the war ended. A musket ball had embedded itself in his left hip and had been removed, but he couldn't march or walk without a cane. Caleb returned home in the summer of '65, a young man of twenty-two with an old soul and upon his arrival he found his childhood house and farm deserted. His mother and father had passed while he was serving and his cousin had sold off the animals and paid the taxes on the land.

Hurting badly from the shock of the death of his parents, he called on his fiancée. They had written each other regularly during the war, although the delivery had been irregular. The last one from her had come not four months before he got home, just before the official end of the war and it had been full of love and longing. Thoughts of her and their life after the war had kept him going in his darkest hours.

He was so full of anticipation he thought he would burst, when he had called at her parent's farm. They had met him with solemn expressions. Fear cascaded through him, as he thought something bad had befallen her, but her father stepped out and as they walked, he told Caleb what had transpired in his absence. His fiancé had met and married another young man, a bank clerk. A good man, the father proffered no blame to anyone, telling Caleb things usually worked out as they should. Caleb, in shock, had thanked the girl's father, smiled, shook his hand and walked away. He felt hollow, as though his soul had left him. He made no attempt to see his former love. His absence had been too great a burden, she must have been terribly lonely, he thought.

Caleb's inheritance was limited to the family's small farm, without any animals or implements. He managed to get a small operation going and gave it his all for three years. He had grown up farming, but found the constant battle with prices, insects and the weather to be too frustrating. The farm had sold quickly, but after he paid off his debts for seed, equipment and animals, there was precious little left.

With nothing to hold him, haunted by the horrors of the war and hurting from the shock of his fiancée's change of heart, in the summer of '68 he had ridden out of Ohio. He had always loved horses and could ride with the best, so finding himself in Texas at a time when rounding up longhorns was popular, he had hired on and found it easy to adapt to cowboying.

The long days and hard work helped him not to think about his past, but he had trouble sticking anywhere and four years after he rode out of Ohio, he found himself in Mexico, enjoying the people and the food.

One day, having left a ranch in southern Mexico where he had worked for nearly a year, he rode out seeking new surroundings. He noticed a large ranch house and bunkhouse on a hill and rode up to the casa and asked for work. He had picked up some Spanish in Texas and being in Mexico had improved his vocabulary, although it didn't take much to master the words he needed to get by. Everything he owned was with him. He needed to earn some money and figured he'd work a month and move on once he was paid. However, after he signed on, he met another American, Billy Ray, who everyone called B.R.

B.R. had been working at the ranch for nine months and besides speaking English, had a working knowledge of Spanish. There was a stark contrast in the two men's appearance. Although both were in their early thirties and lean as willows, B.R. was dark-haired and brown-eyed; his dark hair falling just over his ears. Unlike most men, he preferred to be clean-shaved. Caleb was fair, with long blond hair that fell to his shoulders and he sported a blond mustache and a light beard. His blue eyes changed hues with the light. The two found they enjoyed each other's company and their histories were eerily similar. Both had served in the Civil War, and both had loved and lost. Both men had worked and drifted since the war, not able to find their place in the world. Caleb, having no place to be, stayed on. He had been there three months and B.R. a year on payday. After drawing their wages, they looked at each other and knew what the other was thinking.

The next morning, early November 1874, after breakfast, they said their goodbyes, shook hands all around and rode for Texas.

Chapter 4

Johnny and Rosalinda were sitting by the fireplace, reading by lamplight. Johnny was studying a week-old copy of the San Antonio Daily News. Rosalinda was engrossed in an article in a magazine that appealed to women readers, *Godey's Lady's Book*. Her friend Martha had obtained a copy of the monthly which was published in Philadelphia and loaned it to Rosalinda, who was so taken with it, Johnny purchased a subscription for her.

The magazine had articles written by both men and women, but each month it contained information on the latest fashions and a new sewing pattern. As he read the Daily News, Johnny noted there seemed to be more ads than news, but he read the ad for new Moline Plows made by Deere & Company. Henry had been repairing their plow every few weeks it seemed. Maybe, he thought, he would have Henry take a look at plows the next time he went to San Antonio. There were several ads telling folks they could work from home and make up to thirty-five dollars a week. This seemed unlikely to Johnny.

As he scanned an ad that offered pasturage for horses at two dollars a month, another ad, a very small one, caught his eye. An auction at a ranch was set for December 12, 1874. The ad stated that hundreds of pieces of farm equipment, tools, and tack, would be offered. Additionally, as a bonus, a number of horses, including stallions, from various parts of the country would be offered. What captured Johnny's attention was a note that among the horses for sale were two Percherons, a filly and a mare, recently imported from France. The idea of finding a mate for Loco fascinated Johnny. The sale site was in New Orleans and the sale date less than three weeks away, but Johnny felt a strong urge to go.

New Orleans. It had been years since he was there. He was sure Rosalinda had never been. Maybe the two of them could travel out there; tour New Orleans and visit the sale. The more he thought about it, the more he warmed to the idea. Even if he didn't buy a horse, it would be an adventure for the two of them.

Running the logistics through his mind, Johnny knew it was possible to reach Galveston by train, although they would have to board the train in Waelder, Texas, about a hundred miles, he estimated, from his ranch. Once they reached Galveston, they could catch one of the mail boats that went to New Orleans. If he purchased a horse or two, they could arrange transport for the horses and themselves and backtrack the same way. Well, at least it sounded reasonable, although he admitted to himself, he had never been on a train. Smiling to himself, he decided he would discuss the numbers with Rosalinda. She had proven to be a master at the business end of numbers and money.

He laid the paper on the hearth and looked at Rosalinda, watching her read. How he loved this woman, he thought. Rosalinda, as though she felt him looking at her, looked up and her face broke out in a huge smile. Johnny could hardly catch his breath.

The two looked at each other for a minute, then, finding his voice, Johnny said, "Rosalinda, I saw a notice in the paper about an auction. There will be some horses, stallions up for sale and two mares; Percherons. I thought I'd get you to look at the costs of adding a horse or two, if you think it would work out."

Rosalinda looked puzzled, then replied, "Have you already forgotten? We did that a month ago. It would be a good investment."

Grinning, Johnny said, "Well, the sale is in New Orleans, so there would be expenses, traveling and transporting the animals."

"New Orleans!" exclaimed Rosalinda, clearly surprised.

Quickly, Johnny added, "I thought we'd both go. It's been forever since I've been there, and I thought maybe you would like to visit New Orleans. It's a fascinating place."

Processing this unexpected idea, Rosalinda bit her lower lip, as she sat, studying her husband. Johnny, gaining experience at being married, kept quiet, letting Rosalinda think.

After a few minutes, Rosalinda said, "Johnny, I would love to see New Orleans, really I would, but since we're on the subject, it has been a wish of mine, to visit New York or San Francisco."

Johnny studied his wife's face, as it was his turn to be surprised. "I don't think you've mentioned it," he finally uttered.

"I haven't," she said. "It's something that, well, I guess it's the pictures and articles in the magazines. It's like a different world. Every woman would probably like to see New York. I'm sure New Orleans would be very interesting, but what I'm trying to say is, I think you should go. If you find suitable horses, the cost of transport won't be a problem. And besides, Lucrecia is learning her numbers. She and I will wait here for you."

Johnny, now, on unexpected and unfamiliar ground, studied Rosalinda, trying to figure out what it all meant.

"Well," he said.

"Johnny, I truly appreciate you offering to take me with you, but as you know, we've been saving money each month and maybe if things go well, next summer we could go somewhere."

"Ah… maybe we could go to New York," said Johnny, the idea just occurring to him.

"That idea excites me a great deal," said Rosalinda. "And I would want to take Lucrecia if we could."

"Of course!" exclaimed Johnny, smiling.

Later, in bed, exhausted, but happy, Johnny wondered if going on a trip to New York had been his idea or Rosalinda's. He wasn't sure. Somehow he had committed to it without even giving it much thought. Smiling to himself, he considered that it was something he probably should have thought of, but he still didn't have a handle on how women thought and he probably never would. In minutes, he was fast asleep.

The next morning, when Johnny tried to explain to Henry Bear how he had worked out a plan, in his mind, to take Rosalinda to New Orleans and while there to attend an auction. But somehow he had ended up committing to taking her and their daughter to New York next summer. Henry broke into uncontrolled laughter.

"I don't see how you think this is funny," said Johnny. "It's confusing is what it is."

"Oh, I'm not laughing at you Johnny, you know, it's just funny cause I think if Ms. Rosalinda just flat out asked, you'd a thought of a reason not to agree, but, fact is, you'll be going to New York."

Johnny looked at Henry, suspicious that he was making fun of him while pretending not too, "Did I see you out clearing the ground for a Spring flower garden the other day?"

Henry, looking sheepish, said, "Oh, yeah, I had a little time, so I worked on that for a bit."

"Hmm, didn't you tell me Venus wanted you to do that, but you told her you weren't gonna do it until closer to Spring?"

"Yes sir, that's what I said. I told the woman it would have to wait, and seeing how I'm the man of the house, she didn't argue."

Johnny pulled a cigarillo out of his pocket, found a match, lit up and looked at Henry once again, but didn't say anything.

Henry busied himself digging his tobacco pouch out of his jacket pocket and filling his pipe. Then, looking over at Johnny he said, "Well, the woman asked me again while we was in the throes of passion and I guess I mighta agreed to go ahead with getting the ground ready."

Johnny howled with laughter. "Man of the house are you," he said, trying to control his mirth.

"It ain't fair," said Henry, "her pressing me at a time like that."

This statement got Johnny to laughing again, and Henry soon joined in. Two married men, trying to figure out how married life worked.

CHAPTER 5

By early December Caleb and B.R. had worked their way up to San Antonio, finding the weather cold, but clear. They were eating the noon meal, or dinner as it was called in the south, in a small family-owned restaurant on the river, Café del Rio. As they ate and talked, B.R. asked Caleb to accompany him to a ranch east of town, to meet John Christie, the man he worked for before he left for Mexico, some three years before.

"We might be able to hire on there," said B.R.

"Isn't the girl that you," Caleb paused, "sorry."

"It's okay. I'm sure she's married and all by now. I'm over her. It's all in the past."

Caleb looked at B.R., but didn't comment.

Suddenly loud laughter from another table interrupted their conversation. Both men turned to look and saw four men, all about their own age looking at them while they laughed. B.R. went back to eating, but Caleb studied the men. They were pale, their faces fleshy. As he continued to stare at them he noted they were all well-groomed, well-dressed, their clothes and hats devoid of dirt or dust. Their clothes were made of fine cloth, with ruffled shirts and ties. City boys, thought Caleb, rich city boys. Known as dandies to cowboys. The one who appeared to be the leader was, Caleb noted, a handsome sort.

As Caleb turned his head to look at B.R., he smiled. He and B.R. had been living rough and did in fact present a sight. Their clothes were dirty and dusty, they were unshaven, dark and gaunt. The opposite of the soft looking young men who were having fun at their expense.

Their waitress was a girl not much younger than themselves. She had a dark complexion, dark eyes and long dark hair, gathered in a single braid that stretched down her back. They both assumed she was a part of the Mexican family that owned the café. Appearing at their table, she refilled their coffee cups without comment before moving across the room to fill the cups of the four laughing men.

"I need to get Champion's hoofs trimmed and his shoes replaced," said Caleb. "You want to ride on out to the Christie place and visit? I reckon you'll want to stay the night. If you'll give me directions, I'll ride out tomorrow and if they're hiring, we'll be there and if not we can decide what to do."

"That'll work amigo," replied B.R.

The rich boys had stopped laughing, but in the quiet, Caleb and B.R. suddenly heard one of them harassing and belittling the waitress. One of the others joined in as their friends laughed.

"Why don't we step out back, Chica? I'll show you a good time," said the leader, grinning and looking the waitress up and down while he licked his lips.

"¡Solo salgo con hombres! ¡Hombres de verdad, no niños pequeños que se visten como niñas!"

Caleb and B.R. quickly turned to watch the confrontation. Caleb understood only a little of what the girl said, something about real men not boys who dressed as girls. B.R. laughed at the girl's reaction.

"She said she only steps out with real men, not little boys who dress like girls," B.R. explained to Caleb.

"You watch that smart mouth Mex, or I'll bust your teeth out for you," said the leader of the group.

There was silence for a second and in that time, B.R.'s chair scrapped across the floor as he pushed back and rose, turned and headed for the table of young men. He moved so quickly, he was there before Caleb could react and rise himself.

As Caleb stood up, he heard B.R., his voice low, but steely.

"Where I come from, harassing young ladies is considered bad taste," said B.R., addressing the group as the waitress stood, holding the coffee pot, surprise showing on her face.

All four of the young men went quiet, total shock on their faces. Finally, a smirk appeared on the leader's face. "What do we have here boys? Do my eyes deceive me or is there a filthy, stinking, chicken-necked, turd mucker talking to me?" he asked, then looked at his buddies for approval.

"You want somebody to go out back? I'll be glad to step out and teach you some manners," said B.R., through clinched teeth.

The leader's face grew tight, but he didn't respond.

"That's what I thought, big man, you are Mister Brave talking down to women.," continued B.R. "I hear of you bothering this lady again and I won't be asking your permission to school you."

The leader stared, seemingly frozen in place, when one of his friends said, "Whoa," and smiled.

Another said, "What the hell, Reginald?"

It was enough to prod Reginald, the leader of the group, into action. B.R. saw Reginald's eyes go wide and threw his arm up just as the young man grabbed his coffee cup and threw the hot liquid at B.R.'s face. Most of it was deflected by his arm, but B.R. felt some the hot liquid hit his face as he stepped forward and grabbed Reginald by the front of his shirt and yanked him out of his chair with his left hand. As he hit him with his right hand, he let loose with his left causing the man to land on top of the table, sending dishes, food and coffee flying.

One of the other young men jumped to his feet and Caleb yelled, "Hey!"

When the man turned his head, Caleb hit him with a roundhouse right hand that sent him flying back into his chair which turned over as the man flopped onto the floor. A third man had gone to the aid of Reginald who was being pummeled by B.R. The fourth backed up, refusing to join in the melee. The girl had also stepped back, but stood watching impassively.

As Reginald's friend stepped up to help him, Reginald himself crumbled to the floor and B.R. stepped forward to engage the man. The man feigned a right hand and hit B.R. solidly with his left, splitting the skin above his right eye. Blood poured from the wound, entering his eye, effectively making B.R. one-eyed for the moment. The man smacked B.R. twice more, once on the jaw and once in the body. The two grappled and wrestled, knocking over another chair, and falling to the floor, rolling around, before the man broke loose and they both stood up.

Suddenly, lunging forward, the man threw a right hand at B.R.'s jaw, with enough force to finish him, but B.R. got his left arm up and blocked the blow as he hit the man with his own right, then stepped back as the man crumbled to the floor.

No one moved for a moment. The fight over, Caleb righted one of the chairs and B.R. took off his kerchief, folded it and pressed it to the cut on his head. As the fourth man, who hadn't taken part in the fight helped his friends to their feet, B.R. stepped over to the girl and smiled.

"Look what you've done!" she exclaimed. "My grandparents café!"

Stunned, B.R. said, "Well, look, I'll pay for anything that's broke."

"What about the business you have cost us?" she demanded.

"Now look here, lady, I was coming to your defense," lamented B.R.

"I do not need a man to defend me," said the girl, through clenched teeth. She stared hard at him for a moment, and then began to gather the scattered dishes as the men, two of them helped by the other two, left the cafe. There were only four other tables, but they all had customers seated at them, and two of the customers rose and left. Talk resumed in the small dining room at the other two tables.

B.R. and Caleb helped straighten things up and the girl went through a door into the kitchen. A man came out a minute later. He was an older Mexican man and introduced himself as the girl's father-in-law and owner of the café.

After looking around the man said, "The damage is minor, but we can't have fighting. If people hear they will not come anymore."

"I'm rightly sorry sir," said B. R, holding his kerchief to his head. "It just got out of hand. It won't happen again. We're peaceful types, but those fellows was giving the girl a hard time and it riled me."

Nodding, the man replied, "Buena."

"Sir," said B.R. as the man turned away. "Would you please tell the young lady I'm sorry for the trouble? Really, I just meant to help her."

This caused the man to smile. "Others have made that mistake. You are fortunate it wasn't Girasol you tangled with. You'd be needing more than a few stitches. She is my dead son's widow. Her name is Topsannah. It means prairie flower. We call her Girasol."

"Sunflower," said B.R., quietly, to himself.

Noting the confusion on B.R.'s face, the man said, "Her mother was Comanche," and with that, he turned away and went back toward the kitchen, but stopped and turned around. "There's a doctor two streets west and a ways south."

B.R. and Caleb found the doctor and after receiving six stitches, Caleb asked for directions to the blacksmith.

As the two exited the doctor's office, B.R. said, "I'll see you tomorrow," mounted up and headed out to the Christie spread.

Caleb found the blacksmith and after discussing what he wanted done, he asked if he could leave his saddle and tack in the store room. The stable owner agreed and Caleb asked where he might find a cheap room for the night.

Smiling, the man said, "I reckon down toward the District might suit you,"

As night fell, Caleb, walking, knew he was in the right area, west of the site of the Alamo, when he began to see the saloons and gambling houses. He saw women, obviously prostitutes, loitering outside their cribs. A few called to him, but he kept walking. He saw a sign for rooms to rent above a dry goods store. The room was far from fancy, but it was clean. Caleb had learned caution in Mexico and had sewn some of his money into a secret pouch on his saddle. He had some in his boot and a little in his pockets. Texas had outlawed the carrying of guns except for travelers, although some still carried, mainly concealed. But Caleb wanted no trouble, so he left his gun in his room. After coming down the stairs and stepping out on the street, he began to walk, enjoying the cold air and studying the people on the streets, mostly men. Spotting a saloon, he decided he might stop in for a beer or two.

The name above the door announced it as the Grand Saloon. It was crowded and a lively group was crowded around a single faro table. Shouts of victory and curse words of loss erupted with frequency. Caleb pushed into the crowd and, reaching the bar, ordered a beer. He drank it and asked for another. As it was set in front of him, he overheard the two men next to him talking.

The one to his right was saying, "I've never been down into Mexico. I've always wondered what it was like."

"I don't mean to interrupt, but can tell you a little, I've just returned from there," said Caleb, turning to face the man.

The two men, both about his age looked at him. One man responded. "You don't say. Well, what was it like? Are there lots of pretty senoritas down there?" he asked, grinning.

Caleb smiled back. "Oh yes," he said.

"Do any of them speak English?" asked the man serious now.

"Not many," replied Caleb, "but you can get by. There is usually someone who understands a little English and with hand signals and drawing a picture in the dirt if you have to, a man can get along. It gets better after you pick up a little Spanish."

Nodding, the man said, "I'm thinking of going. See the country. Is there work? Cowboy work I mean, I'm no sod-buster."

As they talked, Caleb, never a big drinker, finished his beer and ordered another. He and the stranger talked horses, cattle and Mexico. Before Caleb knew it, he had been there over two hours and realized he was tipsy.

His new friend excused himself and they shook hands. As the man moved away from the bar, his space was filled with a woman. One of those who worked in the saloons.

"Your hair is as long as mine," stated the woman, admiring Caleb's long blond hair and his startlingly blue eyes. "I'm Lila. Why don't you buy me a drink and tell me about yourself?"

Caleb smiled and ordered the woman a drink. He wasn't interested in engaging her services, but she smelled good and it was nice to be close to a female. After an hour, he told her he was going to turn in. She smiled, kissed him on the cheek and disappeared into the crowd, in search of another customer.

As the evening grew late, Caleb pushed away from the bar and eased his way through the busy saloon and out the door.

Caleb came to his senses slowly, as though awaking into a fog. His first impression was a sense of confusion, the second was pain, lots of pain in his head. He was laying in an alley in the dark. A terrible stench was coming from an open window. Some kind of food odor. As he rose to his knees, he vomited. He didn't know how long he had been unconscious. Standing, shaky, he took an inventory of himself. He felt a large lump on the side of his head, and his hand came away bloody. One of his pockets was pulled out. He patted his clothing. All of his money was gone. It hadn't been much, but someone had wanted it bad enough to try to cave his head in to get it. His knife was gone. Fortunately, he had left everything except some spending money in his room or sewn into his saddle. He found his room key still in his vest pocket where he had put it. His hat was on the ground, a few feet away. After recovering it, he walked out to the deserted street and looked around. Leonard's Dry Goods Store, his room above it, was only a block away. Reaching the stairs, he climbed up; fumbled with the key and the lock, and entering the dark room, collapsed on the bed.

CHAPTER 6

Johnny gave Rosalinda and Lucrecia a last hug and stepped off the porch and into a cold rain. It wasn't yet daylight, but he looked back as he climbed into the wagon, Henry already there, reins in hand, ready to go. Johnny looked out toward the barn, but he had already talked to Loco and the dogs and they had all disappeared.

Rosalinda waved as the wagon drove away and Johnny lifted his hand. When the wagon was out of sight of the house, Johnny turned back to face the front and pulled a cigarillo from his vest pocket, cupping it and tilting his head forward, to shield it from the rain. After lighting it, Johnny's thoughts turned to the journey ahead.

On paper, it looked simple enough. He had picked up some train and steamship schedules in San Antonio on Wednesday as he and Rosalinda and Lucrecia were traveling to her parents for Thanksgiving. Rosalinda's father, Lupe, himself a horse trader, was excited about Johnny's trip and the two poured over the schedules, mindful that it might prove difficult if not impossible to reach New Orleans in two weeks or so. It was somewhere in the range of five or six hundred miles.

After some hours at it, the two men developed a plan. Lupe had offered to let Johnny have a horse to ride to Waelder; one he could sell there. The two discussed it and they felt that at thirty miles a day, it might well take a little over three days to reach Waelder. Johnny would need some time to sell the horse. If he left early Friday, he could make it by Sunday night, but it would be a close thing. They decided it would be faster to take the stage. The final plan called for Johnny to take a stage east, toward Houston, leaving on Friday, the day after Thanksgiving. If he could reach Waelder by Sunday afternoon, he could catch a train due to leave that evening. In Harrisburgh, the train terminal just east of

Houston, after a day's wait, he would catch another train; this one going to Galveston. There he would catch a steamship that carried mail and passengers east and would stop in New Orleans.

As they rolled along in the wagon, the rain continued to fall. It had been raining since yesterday and, Johnny was thinking, the roads would be a sea of mud. Stagecoaches were often days late in arriving or completing their runs in weather like this. This rain could last for days. Change of plans, thought Johnny. He would try to buy a horse and ride to Waelder, where, hopefully, he could catch the Sunday afternoon train. He didn't have a lot of room for problems as he had stayed for Thanksgiving and now it was already Friday, November 27th. Well, he thought, he'd make it. He had about two weeks. The problem would be getting back. No matter what happened, he would have to be back for Christmas, so if he included the day of the auction. He would have thirteen days. It would be a close thing, but he felt strongly this was a chance to buy some Percherons.

As they neared San Antonio, Henry, water running from his slicker and hat, turned to look at Johnny. "I reckon you're thinking what I'm thinking."

Johnny nodded. "Yep, the roads are going to be a mess. Stages will be running late if they're running at all. Best take me to Ellison's stables."

Arriving at the stables, Johnny and Henry talked for a minute and then Henry headed back to the Black ranch. Johnny found the proprietor and asked him if he had a solid horse that might make a hundred-mile trip in less than three days.

"I need to be there Sunday afternoon," said Johnny. "I don't reckon the stagecoach will make it in this weather."

Ellison thought a minute and said, "Johnny, I think, with this rain and the roads awash, a mud wagon, with a team, at least four or maybe six horses is likely your best chance. A horse will tire fighting the mud. I don't have one, and I have no idea if he'd be up for it, but old man Jameson quit his mail route, retired he said, a few months ago. If he still has a mud wagon, you could rest the horses and maybe switch off driving and make it. I've let him help me a little from time to time so he can earn a little cash money." He hesitated. "He's an older man, but I reckon he could make it. What he'd want for his trouble, I don't know, but if you're set on going I'll give you directions out to his place and loan you a horse to get you there."

Johnny found Jameson's place and he tied the horse to a tree which offered some protection from the steady, cold rain. He saw an old mud wagon sitting by a small barn. He heard horses' nicker from inside the building. After walking up to the modest house, a cabin really, he knocked on the door and then stepped back out into the rain to wait.

It was a full two minutes before the door opened and a man stepped out on the porch carrying a rifle at his waist, its muzzle directed toward Johnny. The rain dripping from his hat, Johnny studied the man. He was, estimated Johnny, probably sixty or so. An age that to a younger man, would seem ancient. After the stable owner's reference to old man Jameson, Johnny had expected a man of seventy or eighty, but then he should have known better.

"Mr. Jameson," said Johnny. "I'm Johnny Black. Ellison, from the stables, gave me your name and location. I'm looking for a ride to Waelder."

The man held the rifle waist high and studied Johnny for a moment. "Johnny Black you say. You the Johnny Black what was a deputy sheriff over to Medina county?"

"Yes sir," said Johnny.

"Well hell man, don't just stand there in the rain and cold, come on in. I've just made coffee."

The cabin was sparse, but neat and clean. Jameson and Johnny sat at a homemade table sipping coffee.

"I read the San Antonio papers. The stories of your adventures in Medina county were quite entertaining."

Smiling, Johnny replied, "I saw some stories in the paper, but I didn't bother reading 'em. I'm guessing they read like dime novels."

Laughing, Jameson said, "Yep, they kinda did, truth be told. Any no how, what brings you way out here Mr. Black? A ride you say?"

"Call me Johnny if you will and yes, I'm trying to make my way to Galveston and I want to try to catch the train at Waelder Sunday evening. The problem is this rain."

Jameson studied Johnny. "I ain't never been on no train, but I hear they're the fastest, most comfortable way to cover a distance."

"Fact is, I've not been on one myself, but I'm trying to make a horse auction in New Orleans on the twelfth of December. I figure to catch a ship in Galveston. If I buy a horse or two, I hope to bring them back the same way."

Jameson got up, walked to a shelf and returned to the table with a bag of *Genuine Bull Durham Tobacco* and some papers. He began to build a smoke. "You want one?" asked Jameson, holding up the bag of tobacco.

"Brought my own," said Johnny, pulling one of the cigarillos he favored from his vest. He studied it for a moment, noting that it was a little damp. Jameson lit his quirly and then half-standing reached across the table to hold the light for Johnny.

The two men sat smoking for a minute, then Jameson, his smoke held between his lips got up and refilled their coffee cups.

After sitting back down, he said, "What say we get down to business Johnny Black. Time's a wasting. Luck is running your way. I've got a mud wagon and I reckon I've never let a little rain hold me up."

CHAPTER 7

Caleb, as was his habit after years of early calls to breakfast, woke before dawn, but he lay in the bed awhile, still feeling poorly and sore from his night of drinking, the fight and the knock on the head. The sun was up and the early risers had already eaten and were about their business when he found a café not far from his room. His head felt better, but he chastised himself for drinking too much, a rare thing for him, but still.

As he ate, Caleb fished out a small piece of paper. He studied the directions to the John Christie spread B.R. had drawn on it. After a few minutes he felt like he had it pretty well sorted in his head and put the paper away. As he sipped his coffee, he noticed the cook had stepped out of the back and was staring at him. He nodded and the man nodded back.

Caleb paid for his breakfast, rose and stepped out into the morning. It was cold and raining. After studying the streets for a minute, orientating himself, he set off for the stables, but he hadn't gone far when two men stopped him. They were both wearing badges.

"Morning," said the larger of the men.

Thirty minutes later Caleb was sitting in a jail cell.

He had accompanied the sheriff and his deputy to the sheriff's office for a few questions. Caleb was sure it was about the fight with the rich boys at the Café del Rio the day before.

After ensuring Caleb had no weapons, the sheriff offered him a cup of coffee. Caleb was sitting in a chair in front of the sheriff's desk; the deputy standing behind him, leaning on the wall.

Caleb declined and the Sheriff, smiling asked, "You new to San Antonio?"

"Yes sir," replied Caleb. "I reckon them rich boys complained, but."

Interrupting him, the sheriff asked, "Where are you staying?"

Caleb, a little confused by the sheriff's questioning, told him everything that had happened since he and B.R. had arrived in town. He figured it was the quickest way out of here; just clear it up and pay a fine for disturbing the peace if it came to that.

The sheriff listened, then nodded at the deputy, who left.

"You didn't mention visiting with a young lady at the saloon," noted the sheriff.

"Well, yeah, a girl, Lila, I think her name was, I, ah, bought her a drink and we visited, but I didn't engage her services, so if there's a law against that."

"Where did you go after you left?" asked the sheriff.

"I told you Sheriff, I was on the way to my room, but somebody whacked me on the head and took whatever money was left in my pockets and my knife. When I came to I went to my room and went to bed. Alone."

The sheriff studied him.

"I don't think I should have to pay a fine for something I ain't guilty of," said Caleb, becoming angry now. Then, looking at the sheriff, he continued, "Okay, I reckon the judge ain't available so I can just pay you my fine, is that it?"

"No, that isn't it. You're under arrest for the murder of Lila Jennings. We found her body this morning where you left it after you stabbed her to death. We got a witness. Saw you running away from the body."

Caleb's mouth opened, but no sound came out.

After three days and no word from Caleb, B.R. told the foreman he needed a day. He rode into town and found the stable where Caleb had left Champion. The farrier told him that a deputy sheriff had been there and poked through Caleb's gear and told the farrier that Caleb was in jail.

"I'll sell his horse and tack, he doesn't come pay me after thirty days," stated the farrier.

B.R. paid him up to date plus two days. "I'm going to go see what's happened," said B.R. "We had a little run-in with some rich boys and I reckon they've complained, but if need be, I'll come by and pay for more time."

"Could be, but the deputy said he murdered a saloon girl."

"The hell you say?" exclaimed B.R. "No, no. Somebody's confused. I'll be back."

B.R. mounted his horse and headed for the county jail.

CHAPTER 8

Johnny was familiar with the celerity or mud wagons as they were commonly known. They usually had extra wide wheels topped by iron. Canvas was stretched over wood struts to form a roof and a cover for the sides. They were light and provided a very rough ride, but they could usually make it over muddy roads.

After meeting Jameson at the stables, Johnny put his bag, which included a change of clothes and his gun belt, bedroll, and canteens in the wagon, pulled by four horses. He placed his rifle under the front seat. Jameson had already placed his kit, bedroll and rifle in the back of the wagon, and he wore a gun belt and a knife. Johnny studied him a moment, noticing the gun.

"Old habit," said Jameson, seeing Johnny looking at him, then Jameson shook the reins, yelled "Giddy-yup!"

With that, the wagon charged off in the mist of the cold rain, Johnny bouncing on the seat beside Jameson, who appeared to have taken on a new energy after being called to action.

"I used to drive for twenty hours or more, but I reckon if you could spell me now and then."

"Yes, for sure," responded Johnny.

"With any luck we'll make 'er in twenty-four hours or so travel time. These horses are used to pulling in all conditions. I figure we go maybe eight hours and then rest the horses. The load is light, but we'll need to rest 'em, four times say. Give you six or eight hours to spare, getting you there noon on Sunday, and we'll do better if the rain stops."

The rain was intermittent, but the cloud cover was thick, giving the night an early arrival. They pushed on, but when the two men had been on the road for ten hours, eating jerky as they rode, stopping only once to rest the horses and visit the bushes, Jameson began to look for a place to stop.

Seeing a projecting rock formation that gave some shelter from the rain, Jameson said, "Reckon let's stop for a spell, let the horse eat and sleep. Catch some shut-eye ourselves."

As Jameson unhooked the horses and tethered them in the grass, Johnny searched for some dry firewood. An hour later the two men, having eaten and drank some coffee, slept.

At first light, under a clearing sky, the two men roused themselves, broke camp and continued the journey. They were able to water the horses at a small creek and although it was cold and cloudy the rain had, at least for the moment, stopped.

Johnny offered to drive awhile and Jameson readily agreed.

It was one of those things that can make a difference in a life's path. They had been back on the road for twenty minutes when they rounded a curve in the road, both sides bordered by rock formations some fifteen feet high, when a single shot rang out and Jameson jumped, yelled and dove out of the wagon into the mud. Even before Jameson jumped, Johnny had heard the crack of the rifle and brought the horses to a halt. It was this sudden stop that may have saved his life. As he pulled the reins, he dropped below the curved wood foot panel in front of him just as the rifle sounded again and the board which only seconds ago, Johnny had been leaning his back against, spew splinters as a round punctured it.

Years of experience in the war and in dealing with men with hostile intent took over. Johnny's left hand found the rifle mounted under the foot board and without hesitation he jumped out of the wagon and then rolled back under it as a third shot rang out. He looked, but didn't see Jameson. The horses, the reins slack, began to drift toward the grass on the side of the road. Johnny, in a sudden and violent movement, rolled to his left, covering himself in mud, and rolling into six inches of water and high grass before scrambling up and behind a large boulder just as the rifle cracked again.

Johnny studied the area and still couldn't see hide nor hair of Jameson. Where had the man gotten to? Some small rocks, disturbed by someone or something, slid down the embankment across the road some thirty yards away. Whoever was up there was changing his position, trying to get a clear shot at him and Jameson. His mind shifting from immediate action to tactical considerations, Johnny removed his hat and sat it on the rock beside him. Thankfully, it wasn't raining at the moment. He took out a cigarillo, pleased it wasn't crushed, lit it, drew deeply and sat it beside his hat. Then he crawled to his left up through the rocks and vegetation, careful to move slowly so that there was no movement in the brush.

Another shot rang out, but this one was farther away, higher. There were at least two of them considered Johnny. Reaching the highest point on his side of the road, Johnny crawled toward the road, keeping low. He peered through a large scrub brush and saw movement at the top of the rocks on the opposite side. He didn't have a clear shot, so he waited. His looking glass was in his bags in the wagon. A bit of a stalemate, he thought. If the highwaymen moved down to the wagon, he would have a clear shot. But the same thing applied if he went back down. A waiting game.

Five minutes passed. Johnny was wet, muddy and cold, but his mind was focused. This was a game, but a serious game. A game of life or death. He considered the situation, his mind working quickly. It was obviously a robbery and likely that the highwaymen thought this was a mail run which sometimes carried valuables. It would have, thought Johnny, been easier for the outlaws to approach the wagon on horseback, get up close, and pull their weapons, but then again, many men had died in close encounters. There were likely two men, he decided. Cowardly types who figured they would kill from a distance and then rob the wagon without any risk to themselves. One was still up high, providing cover while the other one tried to flush them out or get the horses to move down the road so they could take the wagon and its contents.

Noticing movement again, as someone worked their way down towards where the horses and wagon sat crossways in the road, the horses grazing, Johnny decided to take some action. It had always been his preference to take the fight to whomever he was at odds with and this would be no different. He wondered if Jameson had been hit. If so, he was likely dead or dying in the bushes on the other side of the road.

Suddenly a man ran across the road and scrambled into the brush and rocks. Johnny watched, and decided this was a third man, judging from the place he had appeared. Johnny listened as the man climbed up close to where Johnny had left his hat and a burning cigarillo. Slowly, he worked his way over so that he could see the man. Sure enough, a man holding a revolver was crouched behind a large boulder and began to lean so he could see the spot where Johnny had been.

The man appeared to be tensing to make his move when two shots rang out, so close together the sound came at almost the same instant. The shots had come from across the road. The man froze, listening. Johnny watched him. I wonder if they found Jameson and shot him, thought Johnny, even as he leveled the rifle and stepped out to brace the man near him.

"I wouldn't move if I were you," said Johnny calmly, but with authority.

Whirling to face Johnny, his face a mask of surprise, the man fired, the shot going very high.

He didn't have a chance to fire a second time, as Johnny, holding the rifle at waist level, shot the man in the chest.

Dropping his revolver, the man clutched at the hole in his heart, gasped and keeled over.

"I don't take kindly to someone intends on killing me," said Johnny to the man.

Two more gunshots rang out and Johnny looked out over the road and saw a man on a horse hightailing it down the road, urging his horse into a dead run in spite of the mud. That would be the sniper, thought Johnny. So, he asked himself, where was the third highwayman? After recovering his hat, with great care he began to work his way back down to the road, only to catch a glimpse of Jameson's hat moving in the trees.

"Jameson, that you?" yelled Johnny.

An hour later, the two men stood at the wagon, smoking. Muddy, wet and cold, but happy to be alive. They had hidden the dead men's guns and covered their bodies with rocks to protect them from animals.

"I had to dispatch the fellow," said Jameson without preamble. "I had him covered, told him, but when I stepped out, he turned and fired at me."

"Well, if he was a better shot, you'd likely be dead 'bout now," replied Johnny.

"That's the truth. I just never took no joy in killing," said Jameson, shaking his head. "I've had to in skirmishes and twice running the mail. Well, I reckon we better get moving. I'll have to clean my revolver now," he complained, causing Johnny to smile. "Any no how, we passed Sequin, Texas two or three hours ago, but I figure we're still in Guadalupe county. At the next town we can send somebody to tell the county sheriff what happened and where to find the guns and bodies."

CHAPTER 9

B.R. had found Caleb in jail, and after the sheriff's deputy on duty gave him a brief explanation, he was allowed to talk to Caleb, who told him the story. B.R. was having trouble getting his mind wrapped around it.

"They're telling me there won't be no bail, because it's a murder charge and on top of that I'm a drifter, according to the sheriff," explained Caleb. "Listen, I've got some money, sewn into a hidden pouch in my saddle. Can you fetch it and see about hiring me a lawyer?"

"Of course," said B.R. "I have some cash, so I'll see to it and you can pay me back as soon as they clear this up."

B. R. rode back out to the Christie spread and asked Mr. Christie for a lawyer's name for a friend of his, he explained.

Three days later, the lawyer sat in the cell with Caleb, his face serious. "Your friend, Billy Ray hired me to represent you."

Caleb said, "Howdy."

"No surprise Caleb. The Grand Jury indicted you on a murder charge. I'll have to talk to the district attorney, but your trial will probably be soon. Maybe a week or two. He's looking to have you hung."

Caleb stared at the lawyer. His face giving away nothing. He had already explained, pleaded and cursed. He was beyond that now.

"Our only chance is to mount a vigorous challenge of the witness, but frankly, Caleb, it doesn't look good."

Caleb just nodded.

"I'll be in touch," said the attorney, rising and calling for the deputy.

That night, Caleb sat in the dark, his mind flooded with memories, thoughts and questions. He could hear the deputy snoring. The man came on duty at eleven at night and began drinking almost immediately. He fell asleep every night, but was always awake when a deputy came to relive him about six.

Two days later, the lawyer returned and told Caleb he had questioned the witness and the man seemed to be an honest upstanding citizen. He insisted he saw Caleb or his twin running from the alleyway. 'It was hard to miss the long blond hair,' the man had stated.

So, thought Caleb, maybe there is somebody about with long blond hair like mine. If only I could find him.

Caleb's attorney told him the trial was set to begin in one week and maybe Caleb should consider getting his affairs in order.

He was at his lowest point two days later, when, in a fit of anger he had banged and banged on his cell until the old deputy came and took his chamber pot which stank. Clearly drunk, the deputy didn't return with it and Caleb thought to yell at him when he noticed the man had left the keys in the cell door. Running wasn't his way. He was one to face things, but after a moment's thought, Caleb opened the door, stepped out and peeked into the office. The deputy was asleep, a half empty bottle on the desk.

With nothing to lose, Caleb pulled off his boots, and eased into the office. One of the keys opened a drawer and Caleb found the money he had been carrying in his boot. He left the keys, stepped out onto the porch, pulled on his boots and headed for the stables.

He had to wake up the young man at the stables, telling him to unlock the tack room so he could fetch his tack. The man was very hesitant, but Caleb showed him a receipt B.R. had given him a few days prior, showing he was paid up for his horse's care for another few days.

"I can't give you no refund," stammered the youngster.

"None required," said Caleb.

In minutes he had saddled Champion, given the young man a dollar and ridden out.

Chapter 10

Johnny and Jameson sat in silence as the mud wagon rocked, slid and rolled along the muddy road.

Because of the delay, Jameson was pushing the horses a bit. Johnny touched him on the shoulder and said, "It's okay. No need to press the horses."

Jameson looked at him, nodded, eased the horses a little, and said, "You've a soft spot for horses I think."

"Animals in general I guess," responded Johnny.

After fifteen hours of actual travel, Jameson, who had mentioned at some point that he had traveled this route 'a time or two', studied the landscape and said, "I reckon we're four or five hours out."

Looking at his pocket watch, Johnny noted that it was almost ten o'clock in the morning. If all went well, he would be at the train station by two or three and would easily make the six o'clock train. It had been a tiring journey and after the excitement of the shootout with the highwaymen had worn off, they had both been tired to the bone. Johnny was looking forward to sitting on a train and watching the land go by.

They were moving steadily when a figure broke from the brush on the side of the road and stumbled out in front of the wagon, causing Jameson, who was driving the team to pull them to a sudden halt. Only ten feet separated the team and the figure who had fallen, trying to get out on the road. Jameson and Johnny's first thought was that it was a deer, but quickly realized it was human.

"What the devil?" exclaimed Jameson out loud as he handed the reins to Johnny and stepped down out of the mud wagon, automatically drawing his side arm and cautiously approaching the figure laying in the road.

Suddenly, after turning to look at the approaching Jameson, the figure lurched to its feet and began to stumble across the road and into the brush.

Jameson looked back at Johnny who had lit a cigarillo and was watching the events unfold. Sensing no danger, Jameson shoved his revolver back in its holster and stood watching the figure who had made it to the brush on the other side of the road, but had again fallen.

"Sir," said Jameson. "If you need some assistance you'd best speak up. My passenger is trying to catch the six o'clock train in Waelder and we need to be on our way."

After a moment of silence, a woman's voice said, "Will you give me a ride to Waelder?"

Jameson looked at Johnny who nodded. "Sure, but you need to come on."

A woman, wearing men's clothing and a man's hat emerged from the road. Her face was dirty and scratched from thorns. She appeared exhausted. Slowly, hesitantly, she moved to the wagon and Johnny reached down and gave her a hand up. A small bag hung from a strap around her neck.

With the woman sitting between himself and Johnny, Jameson clucked at the horses and shook the reins. The wagon rolled forward. No one spoke for an hour, and Jameson and Johnny were both taken by surprise when the woman spoke.

"Thank you for the ride. There are men after me."

Johnny and Jameson were silent.

"I can guess what you're thinking. Nothing was stolen, in fact, I haven't done anything to them. I overheard some things, some things involving business and they're afraid I'll repeat it and it will hurt them. So, they'll see me dead if they can."

This statement caused both Jameson and Johnny to look at her.

Finally, Jameson said, "Where did you appear from ma'am?"

"Mule Creek, well, it's called Howard now, I guess. They've opened a post office."

Jameson nodded. "I heard tell the railroad would be coming that away."

The woman looked at him; studied his face, but didn't respond.

When they stopped to make coffee and eat, Johnny studied the woman. Under the scratches, dirt and men's clothing he realized was a striking woman of perhaps fifty, give or take. Stepping away, smoking, Johnny looked back and took note that Jameson had certainly taken an interest in seeing the woman was as comfortable as possible. He had wet his kerchief and given it to her to wash her face and made sure she had coffee and food before he fed himself. Johnny smiled.

The three made Waelder at just past four o'clock and pulled in when they spotted a stable. It only took a minute for Jameson to make arrangements for the horses to be watered, brushed and fed. Johnny asked after the train and was told it was sometimes on time, sometimes not. The woman, who they assumed would disappear, stood silently by, listening and watching. The three were allowed to wash up and using a stall they changed out of their muddy clothes.

Jameson explained that they were attacked by highway men over in Guadalupe county. After offering pay for someone to ride back to Sequin and explain it to the sheriff there, the stable owner volunteered his son. The lad, a young man of sixteen, listened carefully to the story, and map in hand, as well as Jameson's name and address, in the event the sheriff had questions, rode for Sequin.

The stable owner gave them directions to the one restaurant in the town and Jameson, somewhat startled, seeing the woman in a dress, invited her to join them.

"It's my treat," he said smiling to the woman.

For the first time since they had met her, she smiled herself. "My name is Stella, what's yours?"

Jameson said, "Horace, Horace Jameson."

As the three approached the restaurant, the woman took an audible sharp intake of breath even as Johnny took notice of the reason.

Three rough-looking men stood across the street staring at them. All wore holsters and handguns and two had large knives strapped to their legs. Johnny took them in with a glance.

As they ate, Johnny felt like he was alone. Jameson and Stella had, slowly at first, but then more naturally, began to talk quietly. Johnny saw Stella reach over and touch Jameson's arm in a show of affection.

Johnny, finished, excused himself and stepped outside to smoke. Finishing up a cigarillo, he stepped back inside, paid the bill and walked over to the table where Horace and Stella were still talking.

"I've settled the fare," said Johnny. "I'm going to walk on over to the stop and buy a ticket."

Jameson and Stella looked at each other, then Jameson, said, "Johnny, Stella is thinking to get on the train herself and uh, well, I never been on no train, so uh, I was thinking I might leave the wagon and horse at the stable or a wagon yard and go myself."

Surprised, Johnny didn't respond. Jameson and Stella studied him.

"Well then, I'll be glad of the company."

CHAPTER 11

Caleb spent the afternoon lying on a small hill, a few miles north of New Braunfels, Texas. The Guadalupe and Comal Rivers in sight, surrounded by trees and brush, he searched the landscape with the spyglass he had purchased in Mexico. He was in survival mode and both his natural instincts and his experience were still dominating his actions and his thoughts. His horse, Champion, grazed nearby and Caleb longed for a smoke or a cup of coffee, but his fear of capture and his discipline kept him from lighting a quirly or building a fire for coffee. At any time, he might spot the dust kicked up by a posse or see riders in a break among the trees. He didn't have a plan except to do whatever he had to do to avoid being captured or killed. If it came down to it, he already knew he would die before being captured. Being confined in the jail cell and been hard on him; he had thought he was going to lose his mind. Spending years in jail wasn't something he could face. Of course, it was likely they would hang him rather than send him to the penitentiary, so there you had it.

As he lay on the hard ground, shivering from the cold, watching, it occurred to him that he had lived his life by the idea of doing your best at whatever job you were at, and with that in mind, if one were to be a criminal, they should strive to be a good one. In fact, as he thought about it, doing a job well was generally in a person's best interest, but for a criminal, well, being good at it was everything.

At first he had just ridden, urging Champ to move with speed as the terrain would allow, then when he had a few minutes to think, he considered that the sheriff and the posse would likely think him to head south, for Mexico. Of course, that would be the smart thing to do, all things considered. With that thought in mind, he had in fact turned south.

However, some six or seven miles south of Austin, he had crossed a small creek, rode up a way, and coming to some hard ground, turned and rode Champ back into the creek and left Champ in the water. Climbing out carefully, he cut a willow branch from the creek and starting high, he walked backwards, rubbing out his horse's and his own foot prints using the willow branch. Done, he climbed into the creek, remounted and rode down the creek. It wasn't long before his legs and feet were numb with the cold. After working his way up the creek some hundred yards, Champ swimming twice as they came to deeper holes, he threw the branch away. With some luck, the sheriff would pick up his trail, then lose it, and think he had made good his escape and gone to Mexico.

He thought to get up out of the creek, but the banks quickly became steep and he and Champ had to work their way in the water for a good half-mile before they was able to ride up out of the creek and turn back north. By this time, he was very cold, but couldn't risk a fire. It was, he considered, literally a life or death situation he faced.

That night, Caleb, miserably cold, watched for the blink of a campfire, but didn't see one. He watched the trail again the next morning for two hours as he watched storm clouds building in the south. He saw two riders making their way to Austin, and a loaded wagon pulled by oxen, likely a freighter. He didn't see anyone headed his way, so he saddled Champ, mounted and rode southwest, working his way through the trees, well off the main road. An hour after he started, rain began to fall, lightly at first and then in torrents as lightning and thunder filled the sky. He fished his slicker out of his saddlebags and he and Champ kept moving. Late that day, after working his way some twenty miles, Caleb made camp on the north side of the Guadalupe River. The rain had stopped and the evening was turning colder. He wasn't that far from San Antonio, where he had escaped the county jail, but he felt sure he had eluded any pursuit. He rummaged in the saddle bags to see if they had been cleaned out, but surprisingly, no one had thought to or gotten around to stealing his possessions. He was particularly glad to see his coffeepot and coffee along with his tobacco.

After building a fire and making coffee, Caleb built himself a smoke, poured a cup of coffee and set back to consider his options. He had no family, and he hadn't seen any of his friends for years, so he figured he had two choices. The best option, no doubt about it, was to run far and hard, either back to Mexico or northwest, to the territories. A second option was to stay in the area and try to clear his name. It took only a short time for him to decide. There wasn't anything to hold him in Texas, but he would stay and try to clear his name. He wasn't sure why. It was, he reckoned, his pride. The simple injustice of it, an innocent man accused of murder and likely to be hung. It wasn't right.

CHAPTER 12

"We better get on over to the train station," said Johnny.

Jameson took Stella's arm and led her to the right, down the street, the three men nowhere in sight. Arriving at the tiny train depot, the three purchased tickets for the trip to Harrisburgh, just east of Houston. Johnny had strapped on his gun belt and was carrying his bag and rifle. Jameson was outfitted the same, and Stella still had her small bag, a wide strap over her neck and shoulder. She had discarded the men's clothing she had escaped in, including the hat, and now she was hatless, her dark hair pinned up. Johnny was pleased to see the train waiting, its engine running.

The train was due to leave in less than an hour and so Jameson, accompanied by Stella, left to return to the stables to make arrangements for his horses and wagon. Johnny had paid him for the trip and they had shaken hands as though they were going their separate ways.

"I should be paying you," said Jameson, grinning. "A bit of excitement on the road and now I'm going to ride a train."

Johnny smiled and said, "I'll see you on the train." Watching Jameson and Stella walk away, Johnny considered that although Stella and Jameson had hit it off, he felt an unease.

It was the speed of the train that surprised Johnny. It didn't take long to grow accustomed to the sway and clack, clack, clack of the wheels on the track and Johnny could see this was the future. He was a little wary, at least at first, that the speed might cause the rail car to jump off the tracks, but as it sped along, he relaxed. Oh my, wouldn't Lucrecia and Rosalinda enjoy this, he thought, as he watched the landscape roll by. In minutes, his first excitement spent, he began to feel sleepy, the steady clack of the wheels and the rocking motion of the coach putting him to sleep.

Slowing for a curve, the train, consisting of only six cars and an engine, came out of the curve and the engineer saw what appeared to be a wagon on the tracks two hundred yards ahead. Slowly, he pulled back and eased the train to a stop.

Johnny opened his eyes, feeling no great concern, although he had worried some that problems that might delay him. He looked out the window, but couldn't see anything. He turned in his seat to look back several rows, across the aisle to where Stella and Jameson sat. They were engaged in conversation. When Johnny turned back, a man stepped into the coach, gun drawn.

"Evening folks," said the man. "If you want to live to see the sun rise, put your hands on the bench in front of you."

Johnny recognized the man as one of the three that had watched them as they entered the café in Waelder. Slowly, he placed his hands on the top edge of the bench seat in front of him.

"Now, I'm gonna come by and collect watches, rings, money and guns in this here bag," he said, holding out a burlap sack. "Now, if anybody is feeling brave, well, my friend, Rachel; she's the one holding the big revolver in the back there, is gonna blow a hole in you. And that ain't no idle threat."

Johnny turned his head enough to see Stella standing in the back of the coach, a large revolver held in both hands. Jameson, his hands on the bench in front of him, also had his head turned, his mouth open as he stared at the woman he and Johnny knew as Stella, but it appeared, was actually a gang member and train robber named Rachel.

The man worked his way down the train car, but at the third row, a man refused to hand over his valuables and the brigand swung his pistol, the barrel slamming into the man's face, the man yelling in pain. Blood streaming down his face, the man dug out his money. Two rows later, a woman refused to give up her ring and the man twisted the ring from her finger, the woman screaming as the finger broke, then breaking into sobs and wails. The man reached Johnny, who was seated on the right side, about half-way back. As the man stepped up to Johnny's row, he faced Johnny and because there was no one on the left side of the row, he moved close and thrust out the bag. Johnny stared at him grim-faced; rage building in him.

"Let's have it and don't even think about holding anything back cowboy. I'd as soon shoot you as not. Make an example." Johnny hadn't shaved since Friday morning and had slept little. The man looked into his bloodshot eyes and haggard face and relaxed a little. "You a drunk huh," said the man. "I like a drink myself from time to time, old fellow."

Johnny took this opportunity to nod and with surprising violence and speed, he swept his left arm across and caught the man's right wrist, forcing the gun to the side as he half rose and punched the man's throat with his right hand. Johnny grabbed the man's shirt, with his right hand and twisted the gun hand with his left hand, causing the man to lose his grip and the gun to fall onto the bench. With his right arm, Johnny pulled the man downward and to his left just as a tremendous blast filled the car, as the woman, Rachel, fired the heavy revolver. Women screamed, men yelled as passengers in the front part of the coach fought to get into the aisles and out the door.

Johnny let go the man and pulled his own sidearm; the round fired from the women having hit her partner in the side and the man had gone slack and tumbled to the floor. As Johnny lifted his head, he saw the woman disappear through the rear door of the car. Several gunshots, these from another car, split the night with a sharp bangs. Now everyone ducked down in their seats, unsure where the gunfire and the threat came from. Johnny glanced behind him to his right, saw nothing and looked back left toward the rear of the coach and saw Jameson, gun drawn, working his way down the aisle toward the back door where the woman had escaped. Seeing this, Johnny stepped out into the aisle and went right, toward the front of the car. As he recollected, there was only one car in front of them, then the engine. There were, he thought, likely two men in the forward car, one at the front and one at the back although the gunshots probably meant someone had resisted.

Reaching the door, Johnny pushed it open and stepped out on the walkway and cracked open the back door to the forward coach. He could hear women crying and men cursing in a low voice. Someone was whimpering. No one was standing. The smell of gunpowder and fear hung in the still air. He heard a man praying and saw a man's body lying in the aisle, face down, his feet toward Johnny. Judging by his clothing, it was likely one of the outlaws. Blood was seeping from a large exit wound in his back. There were two more bodies. A man was half in the aisle, half in a seat and he was clearly dead himself. Another man was leaning against the window, only his head visible, his eyes closed, he was groaning and talking to someone who wasn't there.

It was clear to Johnny that these two had tried to resist, one shooting at the robber in front, the other taking on the man in the rear. The outlaw in the back was dead, as was one of the passengers. The other passenger wounded, maybe dying, the situation too unsure for anyone to attend to him. Where, thought Johnny, was the second outlaw? His question was answered as a battered, dirty hat rose from the front bench seat by the door, followed by a face and an arm, holding a gun. Seeing Johnny, the man's face showed surprise and he fired quickly, the bullet zinging as it hit something on the back wall. The round from Johnny's revolver tore through the man's head, but he stood, swayed side to side, waving his gun hand, the fingers firmly clenched around the weapon. When a second shot from Johnny's revolver found its mark, it seemed to cut the power to the man's body, and he crumbled.

Running footsteps could be heard pounding across the top of the coach in the eerie silence that followed the gun shots. Looking out the window on the left side of the train car, Johnny saw one of the men he had seen in town that morning ride by on a horse, slamming his spurs into the animal. A body came flying off the top of the train car, landing with a thud in the grass. As Johnny worked his way toward the door, the body rose and stumbled toward the front of the train. It was the woman, Stella or Rachel, whatever her name was. Johnny opened the door at the front of the train car in time to see Jameson, who had climbed down from the roof, where he had sent the woman flying with a running collision; jump down off the train in pursuit of her.

An hour later, they were on their way again. Jameson had tackled and wrestled the woman to the ground and finally was able to subdue and truss her up with help from two other passengers, suffering a bloody nose for his trouble. The conductor took charge and again, with the help of the passengers, the wagon was pushed off the tracks, the dead bodies moved and the wounded man tended to.

Several people thanked Johnny and Jameson for their help, but the pair were reserved and only nodded their acknowledgement. Later, the train rumbling along in the dark, the two smoking, Jameson told Johnny that the conductor told him he heard a woman had escaped from custody in Harwood. A bounty hunter had captured her, having seen her face on a wanted poster for bank robbery. He was going to take her to the sheriff in Travis county.

"I'm guessing those three fellows helped her with the bank robbery," said Johnny.

"I'd be agreeing with your guess," said Jameson. "It's my luck you know. For a while there I thought maybe, well, you know. For some reason, my whole life, I've always been attracted to the wrong women."

Johnny nodded and turned to watch the countryside roll by, considering how fortunate he was, not to have been killed or wounded and thinking a thought that had come to him before, but one he had always quickly dismissed. Texas, so long after the war, was still full of outlaws and danger. Maybe he should move his family to Tennessee or even further north. It sounded like a reasonable thing to do, but he knew Rosalinda would never agree to move so far from her family.

Well, he thought, they were safe enough at home and in the main shopping areas of San Antonio. It would all be okay, he told himself, willing his mind to relax and enjoy the ride.

CHAPTER 13

B.R.'s mouth was open, but he found himself unable to speak. Finally, he managed, "Escaped? What do you mean escaped?"

The sheriff looked at him, his large mustache covering his mouth, his eyes serious. "My deputy made a mistake. Ford took advantage and took off. There's a posse on his trail as we speak. I don't reckon it'll be long afore he's back in custody. That is unless he resists, in which case, he'll be shot on the spot. Might be better for all concerned if he does resist. He wouldn't have to hang and it would spare the county the expense of a trial."

Twenty miles away, the city marshal, a deputy city marshal and two sheriff deputies sat their horses. The assistants and the deputies dismounted and began to look for tracks, cigarette papers, broken branches, anything that might give them a clue as to which way the man, Caleb Ford, indicted for murder, had ridden. A few hours later they found his trail. By the end of the day they knew what he was about. He was headed for Mexico. No doubt about it and it was likely he'd make it. After conferring, they decided to give up the pursuit and inform the sheriff who would inform the district attorney. Hell of a thing, but nothing else they could do.

Caleb, his long blond hair cropped short, using the directions B.R. had given him, rode onto the John Christie spread mid-day and asked the first cowboy he saw where he could find B.R. The fellow looked at him a minute and then smiled, "Oh, the new man, sure, he's helping break some horses down at the lower corral."

After getting directions, Caleb nodded, and said, "Much obliged."

B.R. was standing outside the corral, covered in mud. Standing behind him, Caleb said, "Looks like you got off the wrong side of that mustang."

At the sound of Caleb's voice, B.R. jumped and turned. "Caleb, what the hell you doing here?" he said tersely.

"Well, I'm here to see if I can leave Champion and borrow another horse. I'm going to try to find the low-life what killed that girl, Lila, and clear my name."

B.R. stared at Caleb, his face in torment. "The only thing we can do is talk to Mr. Christie. He's a tough man. Might be he just shoots you or has you turned over to the sheriff."

"I got nothing to lose," said Caleb.

John Christie studied Caleb and B.R. The two of them were in Christie's home office, standing in front of his desk, hats in hand.

"Mr. Christie, this is the fellow I worked with in Mexico, the one I told you about. He's run into a bit of trouble."

Caleb told his story. He explained that he had been indicted, but had not been tried as yet.

Christie sat thinking.

Finally, Christie said, "B.R., I appreciate you bringing this cowboy in, but I ain't hiring right now." Looking at Caleb he said, "Jones, that was a right nice horse you rode in on, an appaloosa it looked like. I consider myself an excellent judge of men and horses. I noticed that horse wasn't branded, I'm guessing he came out of Mexico. I admire a handsome horse. You have a good day."

Nobody moved for a moment, then realization dawning on B.R., he said, "Yes sir, Mr. Christie, I'll just see him to his horse," but Christie wasn't listening, he had already returned to the paperwork on his desk.

Out in the yard, Caleb said, "He called me Jones and Champion ain't no appaloosa." He was interrupted by B.R.

"Come with me. Mr. Christie just bought a string of horses out of Mexico that weren't branded. One of 'em is an appaloosa. I reckon he judged you to be an honest man, but if anybody asks, he turned away a drifter by the name of Jones, riding an appaloosa." B.R. smiled. " We'll turn Champion out and saddle the appaloosa."

B.R. fetched a plate of beans and a cup of coffee for Caleb and the two talked while Caleb ate, standing out back of the bunkhouse.

"What do you aim to do?" asked B.R.

"Well, I'm gonna take a room and visit all the saloons and talk to the working girls while I look for and ask after a man what looks like me, except with longer hair."

B.R. nodded, then said, "I can come in on Saturday nights."

"I appreciate it, but if you got caught helping me."

"I'll take my chances. I'll meet you Saturday night, say eight, in front of the Alamo."

CHAPTER 14

The train made Harrisburgh two hours late, but the train to Galveston didn't leave until the next morning. Jameson had been muted since the attempted robbery of the train, but Johnny, who had already decided the man was more than competent, realized that he was a fighter through and through. Strange, how people thought once you'd reached fifty or so, you weren't capable of doing much. Sort of had one foot in the grave, and a man of sixty, well, young folks generally didn't even notice you. He for one, knew that age meant a lifetime of experience. Older folks, he knew, were often very, very capable. You ignored them at your own peril. If you needed an example, you'd need look no further than Horace Jameson.

The two men stood on the platform holding their bags and rifles, looking around them. Jameson's nose was swollen and the skin around one eye was darkening.

"I reckon I'm for a room, a shave, a bath and some supper," said Johnny. "You care to join me?"

"I think I'm heartbroken," said Jameson, "but a shave, bath and supper, along with a shot or two of whiskey, ought to mend it, and besides, I've heard there're some beauties in New Orleans."

Johnny laughed, and asked, "You reckon that eye is going to give them pause."

"Why no," said Jameson. "I'll explain how I got it in defense of a woman's honor."

Johnny shook his head and the two men headed for the hotel.

The train trip from Harrisburgh to Galveston was uneventful and the two took rooms and began to inquire about passage on a steamer bound for New Orleans. Jameson, having never seen the coast or the ocean was filled with wonder.

As they walked the Galveston wharves, Jameson said, "I been on some river boats, but I don't know about no ship. They say you can't see the land once you're out there on the ocean."

"So they say," said Johnny, his mind on what he had discovered that very day. The Clyde Steamship Line had recently begun to run ships regularly from Galveston to New York. If it proved safe and reasonably comfortable, he would discuss going to New York on a ship with Rosalinda.

The wharves were busy places. Johnny had counted seven or eight ships with cargoes of all types being loaded and unloaded. Coffee, lumber, sugar and cotton were among the goods.

In spite of the cold water, an amazing sight was a number of black men who waded out to the schooners, leading wagons pulled by mules. The cargo was loaded into the wagons for the final trip into shore. Walking back toward their hotel, they noticed the large two-story customs house, work still under way on parts of it, a number of individuals lingering outside its doors. They passed the two-story brick jail, some prisoners standing in the cold air outside. The jail was a depressing site, but the St. Mary Cathedral Basilica stood majestically a few blocks away.

Their hotel was on the 'Strand' as the main business street was called. Jameson had purchased a bottle of whiskey and asked Johnny to join him in his room.

"I've to start a letter to my wife, and I was thinking to clean my rifle and revolver," responded Johnny.

"I'm of the same mind. When you finish your letter, bring 'em over, we can clean them while we have a drink."

Entering Jameson's room, Johnny found a small table had been set in the center of the room, Jameson sat in one of two chairs bordering it. Cleaning gear, two glasses and a bottle of whiskey sat on the table.

"It cost half a dollar," explained Jameson, as he indicated the table and chairs, "but I figured it worth it to be comfortable, sitting and drinking and all."

Johnny placed his revolver, the same Navy Colt he had carried for years, on the table as Jameson poured him a small whiskey.

Jameson eyed the revolver. "Mind?" asked Jameson.

"No, not at all," responded Johnny.

Jameson picked up the pistol and held it, feeling its balance in his hand. He studied it and frowned.

"It's a'61 Navy Colt; with a Thuer Conversion," explained Johnny.

Jameson looked at him, a question on his face.

"With that cylinder in her, she uses metallic cartridges, although I have to load her from the front. I have another cylinder takes the paper cartridges; " said Johnny, then continuing, "if the need arises."

Jameson looked at him. "You know, I'd heard about conversions, modifying old pistols to take the new metal cartridges. What were they called? Oh, yea, Richard-Masons or something like that. Conversions are cheaper than a new revolver I hear tell."

"Yes, enough to make them somewhat popular. The Richard-Masons are a different design, but their conversions for the Navy '61 model didn't begin until, let's see, maybe '71 or '72, I'm thinking."

"I'm guessing it's dependable or you wouldn't be carrying it; or is it new to you?" asked Jameson.

"Unfortunately, it's been well tested. I've been carrying it since early '69. It's serviced me well."

Jameson nodded, and asked, "How's the loading work?"

Pulling a loading tool from a small leather bag, Johnny said, "Let me show you. You have to remove the barrel first."

After demonstrating the loading process for the Thuer Conversion, Johnny asked, "What are you carrying?"

Jameson rose, walked to the bed where his holster lay and slid the revolver from it. "It's loaded," he said, handing the gun to Johnny.

"I'll be hanged," said Johnny, "Colt Peacemaker."

Grinning from ear to ear, Jameson said, "I'm proud of it. Bought her early this year. Cost me nigh on twenty dollars with the holster and some cartridges. Didn't figure to ever need her, but you know, living out in the countryside you never know. I'm glad I been out practicing."

As the pair smoked, sipped whiskey and cleaned their equipment, they talked a little.

"I've always been a Colt man, I guess," explained Jameson. "Carried a Colt Dragoon for many years and then the 1860 Colt Army model till this year." He stopped cleaning, looked away in memory and continued, "Can't rightly remember, but I think it was '52 or '53, I was riding with some fellows. We got in a skirmish with some Comanches. Fellow with us was carrying a Walker. Me and him was penned down and he was so nervous his hands were shaking. He was spilling powder, trying to reload, and finally got it done, but when he fired the damn cylinder exploded on him! Messed his hand up something fierce. The thing is, the Natives disappeared. I've always figured the explosion scared 'em."

Johnny looked up from his work, "I've heard of the Walker's cylinders exploding. Too much powder or sometimes a man, in a hurry, putting the shell in backward."

"Yes," replied Jameson, "I reckon he mighta done both in his state, but we used to put some lard on top to keep that black powder from exploding in all the cylinders at once. He mighta missed that step in his haste."

CHAPTER 15

Caleb found a room in the District. It wasn't much of a room. On the second floor of an old hotel, its better days were long behind it. What made it ideal for Caleb was its location in the middle of what was known as the 'sporting district'. Surrounded by saloons, gambling halls, dance halls and cribs - as the places working girls lived were called. Police were feared and disliked here. Not wanting to call attention to himself, Caleb had left his gun belt with the rest of his gear at the Christie ranch. He had, however, kept his revolver, hiding it under his shirt and had his knife in his boot. When he chopped off his shoulder length hair, he had purchased a new hat from a Mexican street vendor, to alter his appearance a bit more and felt pretty certain he would go unnoticed. There was no doubt; no one expected him to return to San Antonio.

Saturday evening found B.R. taking his supper at Café del Rio. He had two hours before he was to meet up with Caleb. Topsannah, called Girasol by her grandparents, had waited on him, but showed no recognition. She was, thought B.R., as attractive as he remembered her from his only other visit here; the one in which he got in a fight when she was being harassed.

When she stopped at his table to refill his coffee cup, B.R. smiled at her. She looked at him with dark eyes, her face showing no emotion.

"Do ya'll have any pie?" asked B.R.

"Yes, apple," responded Topsannah, who continued to look at him, but didn't respond further.

"Would you please bring me a piece?" asked B.R.

The girl walked away without speaking, returning in a minute and setting a piece of pie on the table in front of B.R.

"I was wondering if you remember me? I was here a while back with my friend."

"Si, I remember. You are the gringo that started a fight in here."

Frustrated, B.R. said, "But I was taking up for you, Topsannah."

The girl's eyes widened. "How do you know my name?"

"Your father-in-law told me. I asked him to tell you I didn't mean no harm. By the way, my name is Billy Ray. Folks generally call me B.R."

"Where is your friend?" she asked, surprising B.R.

"Oh, well, he's, ah, taking care of some business."

After staring at him for a moment, she turned away to check on the other customers.

After finishing and paying for his supper, B.R. stood and waited until he caught Topsannah's eye and, touching his hat, said, "Buenas noches."

Caleb had stayed in his room for two days, only venturing out at night to eat and to purchase a newspaper. No one paid him any mind. One thing he noticed was the large number of Germans, most speaking their native language as they went about their business, but also able to communicate in English. Another odd thing was the number of blacks in the area. In most cases, even though the Civil War was long over, segregation was the rule. But not in this part of the city. Anglos, Mexicans, Asians and Negroes all seemed to blend together. The poor, the rich, the privileged and the outcasts all seemed to blend, although different saloons catered to different clientele.

B.R. found Caleb waiting beside the Alamo and the two nodded to each other.

"I thought to go back to the saloon where I met Lila. Would you be agreeable to asking after her? Might be best if I don't do that myself. If we can find a girl that knew her, maybe they'll have an idea about who she went with that night or if she left alone."

"I'm for it," said B.R. "But let's not drink together. I'll go in first and go to the bar."

"Okay, I'll buy another working girl a drink, ask about 'the girl that was murdered.'"

"Sounds risky Caleb. You know, you could go back to Mexico till this goes away. Folks will forget after a while."

"I know B.R. It just seems, it seems like what I should do."

A half-hour later, B.R. entered the saloon and found a place at the bar. Five minutes later, Caleb eased in the door, worked his way through the crowd and at the end of the bar, ordered a whiskey. After paying, he looked around and took a seat at an empty table in a dark corner.

Caleb studied the men at the crowded bar, and when a man stepped back, he saw B.R. He hadn't been in his seat for a full two minutes when he felt a soft hand touch his neck.

"Buy a girl a drink?" said a voice behind him, as a woman, smelling of rose water, eased into the only other chair at his table.

Caleb smiled at her and took a sip of his whiskey. "Sure."

The girl smiled with closed lips, turned in her chair and the bartender, an experienced man who scanned the room regularly saw her nod and nodded back.

Caleb felt her hand on his leg as she turned back to him. "I'm Mollie," purred the girl.

Studying her, Caleb noted that although she was young, likely in her twenties, and pretty thought Caleb, but her face had a bit of tenseness in it. It was her life in the trade, he thought. It aged the women who made their living in man's oldest trade. He had always had a soft spot for them. It seemed they were all actors playing a part when you met them, but if one ever let her guard down, there was always a story, but never a pleasant one. He had heard some stories of men robbed or duped, one killed, by ladies of the night, but Caleb considered that in society there would always be criminals, some wearing nice clothes, others, well, they could be found in all walks of life to his thinking.

"I'm ah, Cal," he said.

Smiling, Mollie responded, "Cal is it? Well, nice to meet you Cal, and thank you for the drink. You must be new in town; don't think we've met."

"Yes ma'am, just rode in from, ah, Austin."

"Do you mind if I sit and visit a while?" she asked.

"Why sure, I miss talking to females, truth be told."

She studied him for a minute. "So, what brings you to town? You must be a cowboy."

Caleb smiled, sipped at his whiskey. "Yes ma'am. I've been working beeves and horses in Mexico. Are you from hereabouts?"

"No, I'm a small-town girl. Tell me more of yourself."

"There ain't much to tell. I'm just a cowboy, drifting from job to job. Say, I heard tell a working girl was murdered in this part of town awhile back. Doesn't it worry you?"

Mollie's face tightened, but as she looked at Caleb, he seemed to her to be just as he appeared. An innocent cowboy, trying to make conversation. She shook her head.

"Yes, Cal, it worries me, but I try to be careful." She was quiet for a moment, then continued, "She worked here. Everyone was upset. It's different when you know someone who dies."

"Yes, it is," said Caleb, pain in his voice.

"But she wasn't a working girl, or at least as far as I know. The girls that work here, including myself, are saloon girls. We talk and occasionally dance and that's all so if you're looking for something else you need to try another place."

Clearly surprised, Caleb said, "I'm sorry miss, I didn't think and no, no I'm happy to talk. It's my fault for misunderstanding."

She stared at him, unsmiling, trying to judge how truthful he was being and if his apology was sincere. Finally she said, "As long as we're clear."

At the bar, B.R. was engaged in conversation with the bartender and had brought up the subject of the murdered girl. The man enjoyed talking and told B.R. everything he could think of regarding the girl and the night she was murdered.

"The fellow that done it, I knew something was off with him. Had hair like a girl he did. Long and blond."

"So, you saw him huh," said B.R.

"Hell yes, I sure did. Stood right about where you are talking to the girl he killed. I served him and the girl; Lila was her name. She was a purty thing and the most popular girl in the place."

"Dang," responded B.R. "That's something. Did he do it here, up in her room?"

"Nah, girls aren't allowed to take men to their rooms. They're just here for visiting with. He left alone not long afore we closed, but so did she and somebody saw him running and found her body. I'm thinking they were planning to meet somewhere, his room maybe."

Caleb couldn't figure out what to ask Mollie to further his search for the killer. Their talk became general and after a while, Caleb forgot why he was there.

Glancing toward the bar, Mollie saw the bartender giving her a hard stare and she turned back to face Caleb and said, "Cal, if you want to keep talking you'll have to buy me another drink."

"Oh, sure, sure," responded Caleb, quickly.

Mollie raised her hand and in a moment the bartender was at their table with a fresh drink.

Later, in Caleb's room, Caleb and B.R. compared notes.

"Truth be told, I couldn't figure what to ask or how to ask it," said Caleb.

"The bartender was a talking man, but he just told me pretty much what we already know."

"Fine couple of detectives we are," responded Caleb. "I guess my only hope is to visit different saloons and look for a fellow that looks like me."

"What will you do if you find one?" asked B.R.

Caleb stared at him for a moment. "Damned if I know."

Chapter 16

The next morning, Johnny and Jameson stood on the wharf and eyed the Morgan steamer they were booked on. It had a large wheel on one side and featured two tall masts. Johnny reached under his greatcoat and pulled a cigarillo and a match from his vest pocket. As he lit up, he noticed Jameson seemed lost in thought.

After a few minutes, the two men picked up their bags and rifles and with one last look back they stepped on the gangway and boarded the ship. Johnny, in keeping with Rosalinda's habit of watching their money closely, had booked a two-berth cabin for them. Both were surprised at how small the room was and how little space was provided between the bunks on one wall. The rifles wouldn't fit in the small lockers, so the two men ended up laying them in their bunks and tossing the blanket over them. They stowed their bags, with their handguns inside them.

After stowing their gear, they explored the ship a bit and then stood by the rail and watched the shore fade away. The new experience was, at first, interesting, almost thrilling, but it wasn't long before they were out of sight of land and the sea turned into a moving mountain of waves and Jameson found himself clinging to the rail, wet from the spray of the sea and so sick he thought he might die. He wasn't alone, there were many others, heaving their last meals, their faces ashen.

Johnny was so alarmed he sought out a deckhand who laughed. "Tis normal," he told Johnny. "They might get better if the sea calms, but maybe not. It affects some, but not all. We're ninety-five miles from New Orleans and if all goes well will be there in forty hours more or less."

Jameson felt some better after a while and went below to lay in the bottom bunk, but when he began to smell the food cooking in the galley, he hurried back up on the top deck to be sick yet again. Finally, his stomach empty, he returned to the room.

"If I live through this, which I seriously doubt, I'll not be returning with you on a ship," explained Jameson to Johnny.

"I'm told you can expect to live," said Johnny calmly, as though he were discussing breakfast.

Jameson eyed him, looking to see if Johnny was having fun at his expense.

CHAPTER 17

The next week John Christie noticed B.R.'s unhappiness. "You feeling poorly?" he asked.

"No sir, I'm fine, thank you," responded B.R.

"How is that cowboy doing, the one looking for work?" asked Christie, his eyes squinting as he studied B.R.'s face.

"He's at a bit of a loss sir. There's a situation that demands he clear his name, but neither he nor I know how to go about it."

"I see," said Christie, "sounds like he needs a Pinkerton man."

B.R., his mouth open, stared at Christie. "Why that's right," he exclaimed. "How would I find one?" he asked.

Christie sat, thinking. "The expense could be steep."

"Yes sir," responded Caleb. "I understand. My friend has some money saved and it'll not do him any good if he's dead."

"I was just thinking. A year or two ago, my banker mentioned a conman had come to town and made off with some of his customer's money. He couldn't say much, confidences and all that, but as I understand it was a private investigator recovered the money. You might check in with my banker for a name or the lawyer. Lawyers often use investigators."

"Thank you Mr. Christie," said B.R.

B.R. took the afternoon off, even though the foreman warned him his pay would be docked. He found Christie's bank and introduced himself to the clerk. When he asked for the bank manager, the clerk inquired as to his business.

"I'm here on the recommendation of Mr. John Christie, and I would like to call on the manager," responded B.R., sternly.

Shown in to the manager's office, B.R. removed his hat and stated his business.

"You work for Mr. Christie?" asked the bank manager.

"Yes sir," I surely do and I rode with him on a trail drive some years back."

"Of, well then, that's fine. Yes, I did not personally retain an investigator, but I know who you mean and I do have his information. The man offices in Austin."

"Much obliged," said B.R., the name of the investigator in his pocket. He shook hands with the bank manager and leaving, decided to go straight to Caleb's room with the information.

Caleb greeted B.R. with surprise, him coming during the week and during the day, but he was thrilled with the idea of hiring an investigator. They decided B.R. would send the telegram to Austin himself rather than have Caleb risk it. The two men visited a little and then B.R. went to the telegraph office and sent a message requesting the assistance of Dependable Investigations, Attention: Clyde, in a private matter in San Antonio, Texas.

B.R. wasn't sure if he would get a reply today, but he decided to visit the Café del Rio for supper and hopefully, Topsannah or Girasol as she was called by her in-laws, would be working. He saw her just as he stepped into the café and he could have sworn his heart missed a beat. He automatically removed his hat and stood frozen in place. She's beautiful, he thought, standing in the doorway. Finally, realizing she was staring at him, B.R. came to his senses and took a seat, smiling at her as he did so.

She approached him, stopped at his table and asked, "Have you no work?"

"What? Work? Oh, yes, I work as a ranch hand for Mr. John Christie. He owns the Circle C, out east of town."

She stared at him, unsmiling.

"Oh, well, I had to come to town on business."

She continued to stare, finally, she asked, "Do you want supper?"

"Yes, yes," he replied, wondering why his ability to talk had seemed to have abandoned him. He couldn't think. "Anything, anything is fine."

She stared at him for a moment and then turned and walked away. Returning a minute later, she placed a cup of coffee in front of him and walked away again. Ten minutes later, she returned and placed a plate in front of him. He looked at it and saw a mix of beef, potatoes, onions and chilies. There was cornbread on the side.

"Muchas gracias," said B.R. "I love carne guisda con papas."

Topsannah looked surprised, then nodded and walked away.

After finishing his meal, B.R. lingered over pie and coffee, trying to think of something interesting to say to Topsannah. When he had finished his pie and she appeared at his table with the coffee pot, reluctantly, he shook his head no.

"I've gotta get on back to the ranch," he said. When she stood there, but didn't respond, he added, "I reckon I'll be in town for supper on Saturday night."

This brought the tiniest smile from Topsannah and B.R.'s heart sang.

He decided to check in with the telegraph office before he left town and to his surprise a response was waiting. Clyde offered to travel to San Antonio to discuss the situation and cost if B.R. was willing to pay for Clyde's time and expenses. The only alarming issue was Clyde's notice that his fee was five dollars a day besides his expenses. B.R. sent a message agreeing to meet Clyde at the Menger hotel on Saturday evening. He stopped by Caleb's room and told him.

"Well, I hope the man works fast," was Caleb's only comment.

Riding for the Circle C, B.R.'s thoughts and his mood were greatly improved. He was sure Topsannah had smiled at him and now they would have some real help in clearing Caleb's name. He could hardly wait for Saturday.

CHAPTER 18

Jameson finally began to feel better and a calming sea helped. Morning found him at the rail smoking and Johnny joined him.

"You've lost your green pallor," said Johnny, as he lit a cigarillo.

"I'm some better, thank ye," said Jameson. "They say New Orleans is a strange place. You've been there?"

"Yes, I have and it is different."

"Is there drinking establishments?" asked Jameson.

Smiling, Johnny said, "Oh yes, it's not different in that way. Where we have the Mexican and Spanish influence in Texas, Orleans has Spanish and French."

"Do you know the history of the place? I've heard there were a good many plantations worked by slaves. Sugar and cotton I think."

Johnny was silent for a long minute. "Yes, that was true, until the war. As to its history, I understand it was founded by the French in the 1600s, then given to Spain in payment of a war debt in, let's see, I think 1763. Napoleon regained it in a trade around 1800 and as I'm sure you've heard; he sold the entire Louisiana territory to the United States in 1803.

At supper, in the small galley, Jameson and Johnny were joined by a well-dressed man who Johnny guessed to be forty years old or so, with soft hands and a smooth complexion. A banker or lawyer he thought. Maybe a businessman.

"We'll be in port tomorrow," stated the man.

"Can't happen quick enough for me," replied Jameson.

"Ah, your first time at sea," said the man. "It can be a bit rough on a man. I was sick my first time, but haven't had any problems since. I am looking forward to getting home. Is this your first visit to New Orleans?"

"It is for me, my friend here visited some years ago," answered Jameson.

"It's a strange and interesting place, but we did have some troubles a few months ago. Some former Butternuts got it in their head to overthrow the current government. New Orleans is the state capital, so they launched their attack there."

When neither Johnny nor Jameson responded, the man realized they might well be sympathetic to the Confederate cause or perhaps didn't know what a Butternut was. "Ah, some former Confederate soldiers rebelled against the current state government; I think it the best way to phrase it. I think no matter how a man's sympathies lie, it's not in anyone's interest to rekindle the conflict."

"I read a bit about it in the paper," said Johnny, interested. "It lasted for several days, according to the story I read."

Reacting to Johnny's interest, the man continued his explanation. "Yes, the group, they called themselves the White League, were challenging the last election, which of course saw a Republican governor. These folks wanted to install their own man as governor. They support the Democrats and oppose any kind of rights for blacks. It's said they were four or five thousand strong and overwhelmed the police and local militia. They took control of the capitol building, the armory and much of downtown. Held it for several days. Confederate general Longstreet personally tried to stop them and was wounded and taken prisoner."

"How did it end?" asked Jameson.

"Federal troops came in and restored calm. Even though there were killings, so far, no one has been charged. I think the government is hoping if they just let things be there won't be any further trouble. At least not outright armed rebellion."

Although Jameson had barely touched his food out of fear that his seasickness might return, Johnny ate while he thought about what the man had said. It may be years, many, many years before this is all worked out, he thought.

After a few minutes, Jameson said, "Gents, I know politics is a bad subject, but to be frank I'm a little confused by this talk of democrats and republicans. I've always tried to vote for a man based on his merits, but this national stuff is confusing."

Johnny didn't say anything, but looked thoughtful.

The man said, "You're not alone my friend. I daresay few folks really understand it all, but generally, the Republican Party, President Lincoln's party, has turned its focus to business and strength of the national government. They've shown little interest in the black man since the War ended. While the Republican Party is strong in the northern states, the Democratic Party, generally considered the white man's party in the south, is united in their interest in denying the blacks rights, have control of the south and have passed many laws limiting the rights of blacks."

"I see," said Jameson.

"The passing of the Thirteenth, Fourteenth and Fifteenth Amendments to the Constitution have helped of course."

Jameson frowned and the man continued. "The Thirteenth is the one that banned slavery, the Fourteenth guarantees citizenship to all persons born or naturalized here, due process and equal protection of the laws. The Fifteenth says a man cannot be denied the vote based on his race or former status as a slave. Interestingly, the public schools in New Orleans have become desegregated. The white students stayed home for a bit, then came back. I don't know that it will last, but we'll see."

"Thank ye," replied Jameson. "I've not kept up with it all and I understand it a little better."

"The children never seem to see color so much as adults," commented Johnny.

For a few minutes, the three were silent as they thought about the current state of affairs.

Finally, Johnny said, "Can you tell us a little about the city? It's been years since I've been there and I'm sure it's grown and changed."

"Of course," replied the man, "frankly, the city is more like a foreign country than a city, but that only makes it more interesting. It's a mix of Spanish, French, Irish, German, and you get the idea. It is situated on the eastern bank of the Mississippi River and extends to Lake Pontchartrain. We must have close to two hundred thousand souls living in the city. English is of course the main language, but French is spoken freely. Many of the Creoles," the man hesitated seeing Jameson frown, " ah, those of mixed race, live in the French Quarter. There is much trade, due to the port. Oh, you must visit a coffee shop in the Butcher's Hall building on Decatur street. It is like no coffee you've ever had. It's called Café du Monde. They serve a chicory coffee developed during the war. And try the beignets. They're a pastry and very tasty."

"We don't aim to have much time," explained Johnny. "We've come to attend an auction."

"Perhaps I can point you to a hotel close by," responded the man.

Johnny pulled the flyer from his pocket and offered it to the man who studied it.

"Ah, the auction is being held in Algiers on the west bank," he said, nodding his head. The site of a plantation by the way, one of many that is being sold off in parcels.

"Well, I suggest you stay in the American Sector rather than the French Quarter. They speak English there."

Silence followed for a minute as the man seemed to be thinking. "On second thought, the St. James should suit you. It's close to the ferry over to Algiers Point where the auction is and an easy walk or a short ride to the French Quarter where you'll find very good food as well as drinks. If you're of a mind, there is an area that caters to men's more basic instincts."

Johnny smiled and shook his head no, but Jameson just smiled.

"Whatever you do, see a bit of the city. It has a variety of architecture and it's an interesting place. You'll find the St. James on Magazine Street. Anyone can direct you."

After disembarking from the ship, Johnny and Jameson found the ferry and with four hours to spare before the auction began, the two asked for directions to the St. James hotel. Two hours later the two men, having checked into the hotel, left their gear and eaten breakfast, found themselves stepping off the ferry on the west bank of the Mississippi River and joining a group waiting for transport to the auction.

They arrived at the auction almost two hours before it was due to begin and strived toward the buildings and corrals where a large group of men was milling around.

Turning to Jameson, Johnny said, "Thanks again. It's quite a feat, having arrived here in time and much of it is owed to you."

Jameson grinned and said, "I wouldn't have missed it for nothing, well, I could have missed that spell we spent on the ship."

With that the two saw a corral full of horses and men. They made their way toward them. Johnny was thrilled to see not one, but two large horses, sixteen or seventeen hands he guessed, they had to be Percherons.

A large group of men were admiring and discussing them. Jameson and Johnny entered the corral and approached the tall horses. Johnny examined their teeth, ran his hand up and down their legs and examined their hoofs. Jameson was holding one of the horses while Johnny examined her feet, when a man appeared.

"Excuse me," he said, "I take it you gentlemen are new to the area."

Easing the horse's foot to the ground, Johnny straightened up and looked at the man. "How can we help you?" asked Johnny.

Looking very uncomfortable, the man looked about and said, "I'm the agent for the overall sale. I've arranged the auction."

"Pleased to meet you," said Johnny, holding out his hand and the two men shook.

"Howdy," said Jameson, also shaking the man's hand.

"Well, you see, there is something I wanted to make you aware of and you'd have had no way of knowing, if you're not from around here."

Johnny and Jameson looked at the man.

After licking his lips, the man continued, "Mr. Peterson has already said he plans to purchase the two Percherons, and another horse or two."

Johnny and Jameson looked at each other.

"They won't come up for sale you're saying," said Johnny, frowning.

"Well, that's just it, you see, the man that owns the horses is an Englishman and Mr. Peterson made him an offer above his minimum bid for them, but the man is obstinate and insists they go up for auction. I suspect it's because Mr. Peterson is a Frenchman. The English and the French sometimes don't get along."

Johnny waited for the man to continue, then finally the man spoke again.

"You fellows aren't from here. It's obvious from your accent."

"I don't see it's anything to you; if I purchase a horse, I'll be paying in gold coin, not with a draft," said Johnny.

Sighing, the man explained. "Mr. Peterson owns over two thousand acres. A sugar plantation. He's very rich and well, to be frank, it's common knowledge among folks around here it's best not to cross him. He gets what he wants, if you catch my meaning."

Johnny smiled. Jameson frowned.

"He's not the first rich man I've crossed paths with," noted Johnny, amiably.

"Sir, what I'm saying is, it would be in your best interest not to bid against Mr. Peterson. You'd just be driving the price up on him and he won't take it kindly."

With that, the man walked away, only to stop after a few steps and turning said, "You've been warned."

As Johnny and Jameson walked around and examined the equipment and horses for sale, Johnny found three more horses he was interested in. Two were Morgans and the third a strong appearing pinto. Another man was standing close by and watched as they examined them.

"They're fine animals," he said. "Peterson is going to buy them, or at least that was what I was told."

"Peterson, you say?" exclaimed Jameson. "You're the second fellow what's mentioned him. Who the hell is he?"

The man looked around and then said quietly, "He inherited a sugar plantation that has been in his family for nearly sixty-five years. His father died a year or two ago. It ain't just that he's rich, you see. He doesn't hold a position in the Democratic Party here in the state, but he's known to be a powerful man in the party. Behind the scenes like. And well, I've some friends can tell you, if money don't work; he has some rough fellows on his payroll that do his bidding. It's best to avoid him."

The auction began on time and the horses were the first on the block. Several were sold when the Percherons came up for sale as a pair. At the opening bid, a man, tall, slim, gaunt-faced, likely in his mid-thirties, more or less, expensively dressed in what Johnny called 'banker's clothes' with his hair swept back and sporting a thin, dark mustache, nodded and the auctioneer yelled, "We have 300 dollars for the pair of rare horses. Do I hear 325?"

Johnny raised his hand and when the auctioneer acknowledged his bid, the first man to bid, Peterson, turned his head to stare at Johnny, his face a hard mask. He leaned over to speak into a man's ear who was standing at his shoulder. The man nodded and headed toward Johnny.

Johnny watched, waiting to see if there was another bid. Peterson seemed to be surrounded by a small group of hard-looking men. Then he noticed another man, a few feet back from the group. He was an older man, very tall and very heavy. The man didn't smile or talk, but seemed to be observing while at the same time keeping a close eye on Peterson.

"Do I hear 350?" yelled the auctioneer and Peterson nodded.

The man that Peterson had spoken to, arrived at Johnny's shoulder. Johnny looked at him and thought he looked and dressed much like a butler he had seen when he was visiting a rich man in San Francisco with a friend. "Cowboy, Mr. Peterson said he'll give you fifty dollars for your trouble, but he's here to buy the horses, so you must drop out."

This man, sounds like an Englishman, thought Johnny, but he ignored the man and bid 375 dollars.

Furious, the man hissed, "Sir, are you hard of hearing or is it you're just dumb?"

Johnny turned his head and, in a steely, but quiet voice, "Get away from me afore I hurt you."

"It's your funeral," spat the man who whirled and stomped away.

Peterson did not re-bid.

When Johnny bid on the Morgans, Peterson bid a few times and dropped out, and Johnny was the only other bidder. Peterson didn't bid on the pinto and Johnny bid against four other buyers, finally dropping out himself, but he was thrilled to have purchased the Percherons and the Morgans. It made his trip well worthwhile.

Jameson slapped Johnny on the shoulder. "Congratulations. I asked. They'll keep 'em here, but only for a day or two. The fellow here that's in charge of the livestock says his son can move them to the ship, if we tell him where and when."

Johnny smiling, replied, "Good, good. I'm really impressed with the horses. Now, let's get home."

Then, he noticed the man who had offered him fifty dollars to drop out was back where he came from, but he wasn't talking to Peterson, rather he was speaking to the tall, heavy man who listened, but whose face didn't change expression as he looked up and over at Johnny.

Johnny met the man's stare for a moment before turning away and following Jameson.

CHAPTER 19

On the Sunday after the auction in New Orleans, back in Texas, Bear, accompanied by his wife, Venus, drove a buggy into San Antonio and attended the Mount Zion First Baptist Church, a church founded by black members in 1871. They both enjoyed the singing and the congregation's interaction with the preacher's comments. They spent a pleasant half-hour visiting with friends after the service before heading back to the ranch. After returning home, Venus put together a basket of food while Bear unhitched the horses and brushed them down. Then, the two walked out to a favorite place for an afternoon picnic.

Sitting by a fire and enjoying the day, Bear noticed vultures circling in the distance. It wasn't an uncommon site, but there were an unusual number of the large birds and Bear, his pipe freshly loaded, decided to see what they were about after he walked Venus home.

Bear rode his horse, Spartacus up to the carcass of a young longhorn. The vultures moved, but several didn't go far. He dismounted, walked up to the animal's body and kneeled to examine it. The vultures were the last to dine on dead animals, and the body was largely eaten and pulled apart. Maybe a cougar, thought Bear as he studied the remains. But suddenly his blood ran cold and instinctively, he looked around him. He had seen the results of mountain lion attacks on animals twice and this appeared to be something different to Henry. His thoughts ran to stories he had heard as a child, of man-beasts and mystical creatures that haunted the deep woods and mountains.

He looked for tracks, but the ground was fairly hard and he didn't see any.

Bear rode back and went to the main house to tell Rosalinda. There wasn't anything for her to do, but he felt he should inform her. To his surprise, her parents, Lupe and Margarita had arrived to spend a few days and greeted him warmly. When he told his news, Lupe was interested and wanted to ride out and look, so he and Bear returned to the site of the carcass. After studying it a few minutes, Lupe looked at Henry.

"I have seen this in Mexico. It is el lobo. Look here, at the leg bones. See the bite holes in them?"

Henry kneeled down and looked. "A wolf you say?"

"Si. I think there are probably at least two and maybe a pack of four or five. The ground is too hard for tracks, but the carcass has been pulled apart."

"I reckon tomorrow we'll need to try to flush them out," said Lupe. "Otherwise, they will probably kill again. Wolves eat a good bit."

Bear nodded and the two men looked grim.

Early the next morning, carrying rifles, Lupe and Henry Bear rode down to the creek, closest to where they had found the dead longhorn. Here, in the water's edge they found large tracks that appeared to be dog tracks, but Lupe confirmed they were the tracks of wolves.

"Well, we can set traps, or try to find them," said Lupe. "They're a danger to dogs, but I haven't heard of them setting on horses and generally I think they run from humans. I'm guessing, judging by the tracks there may be only two of them. Likely a male and a female. Probably have a den hereabouts."

A quarter mile farther south, Lupe called to Bear and showed him some dung that was filled with hair.

Bear stared at it, frowning.

"Wolf droppings. No doubt about it," explained Lupe. "I remember, we would see wolves hunting and traveling during the day in the winter, but in the warmer months they roamed only at night. I'm thinking these two have mated or will soon. They mate in the winter and birth in the spring."

Low hills could be seen a mile away and Lupe pointed to them. "They've likely dug in on the side of those hills."

Bear nodded and the two men set off in search of the wolves' den. They found a hole in the side of a small hill, just below a rocky formation.

"Looks a mite small for wolves," commented Lupe.

"I reckon a dog could fit in it. Let me pull some of them small rocks loose; widen the hole. Maybe we can see in a little. You reckon they'll come a charging out?"

"Hell if I know," responded Lupe, laughing.

"You stand by, just in case," said Bear, laying his rifle down and clawing at the rocks with a gloved hand. Slowly, he began to enlarge the hole. "Can't see a thing," he exclaimed.

"Fine hunters we are," replied Lupe. "I'm glad Johnny's not about. He be laughing at us."

"What if we get a branch burning and toss it in the hole?"

"Yes," responded Lupe.

The two men built a small fire and spend twenty minutes smoking and enjoying its warmth. Bear, his pipe held in his teeth, picked up a flaming branch, stepped to the hole, leaned over and tossed it into the darkness.

As he reached into the hole and tossed the branch, he thought he saw eyes glowing in the dark. Startled, his pipe fell from his mouth and tumbled into the darkness.

"Oh no!" exclaimed Henry Bear. "My pipe fell in the hole!"

"Just wait a minute. We'll fish it out if nothing is in the hole."

"I think I saw eyes glowing in the dark. Like a cat," said Henry.

The two men watched as smoke drifted out, but nothing came out.

"I'll fire a shot in there," said Lupe, raising his rifle. Close to the hole, he pointed the rifle and fired. The crack of the rifle filled the air, but nothing moved.

"I figured it was too small for wolves," decreed Lupe. "You got a stick or something to fish out your pipe?"

"I think I can get it," responded Bear, laying down and reaching into the hole. After a minute, he withdrew his hand. "There're rocks and sticks in there. It's hard to tell what I'm a grabbing."

He took off the glove on his right hand and once again stuck his arm in the hole. In a moment, he exclaimed, "Got it!"

Just before his hand cleared the hole, Bear let out a yelp and jerked his hand clear. A two-foot, reddish snake flew through the air, landed on the ground a foot to his right and immediately slithered back into the hole.

Lupe, standing close and watching jumped back when he saw the snake. "Snake!"

Bear reared backward and fell over, tumbling down the small embankment. Lupe clambered down to help him.

"It got me Lupe," said Bear, calmly, "but look, I got my pipe."

Lupe looked at Bear, sitting on the ground holding his pipe and grinning. "It was a copperhead, Henry. A den of 'em most likely. I've heard a good many folks survive a copperhead bite, but you're gonna be hurting and weak. We better get back to the horses."

By the time the two men got back to the homestead and told Rosalinda, Margarita and Henry's wife Venus what had happened, Henry was weak, sick and in pain. His hand was swollen. Lupe took off in the small buggy, headed to San Antonio to fetch the doctor.

In bed, a wet cloth on his head and a poultice of wet bread on his hand, Rosalinda and Venus stood by Henry's beside and stared at him. The cats had mysteriously appeared outside the back door and Venus had let them in. They were now on the bed lying beside Bear.

"How is it a grown man sticks his hand into a snake den?" asked Venus, her face drawn.

"I told you, I was getting my pipe," said Henry.

"And here I thought you had some sense," replied Venus.

"We thought maybe it was a wolf den," said Henry.

"Oh, well, that I understand. Sticking your hand in a wolf den. I ain't even gonna tell my momma. I'd be too embarrassed to let her know the man I married ain't got no more sense than a stump."

Lupe and the doctor found Bear weak, sick and in great pain, his hand and arm swollen, but his breathing was regular as the doctor examined him.

"Henry, there're some things we could do. A common treatment for snake bites is to pour ammonia on them and one fellow is recommending injecting it into the blood. Drinking brandy is a common treatment," said the doctor who was interrupted by Henry.

"Doc, what about cutting the bite and bleeding out the poison?"

"A little late for that I'm thinking, but listen to me. There have been several folks bit by copperheads out in the county who had no ammonia or brandy. They just went to bed. But the thing is, all of them, well, least ways the ones I know of, survived. If you're sure it wasn't a rattlesnake, I'm thinking you stay still and you'll live."

Two days later, Bear was better, but still weak. Venus, realizing he was out of danger, had gotten over her anger with him and was now showering him with attention. He was out in the corral, smoking his pipe and watching the young men he had hired brush the horses, when a neighbor rode in and dismounted close to the corral.

"Morning Bear," said the man. "I wanted to thank you for sending the boys over to tell me about the wolves. One of my men shot both of them last evening. They had just killed a bull calf when he happened on them."

"Thank you for riding over to let me know," said Bear.

"They told me you was snake bit. How you getting on?"

"Hurting and weak, but I think I'm going to live, praise the Lord, that is, if Venus don't do me in. She's a mite put out I went and got myself bit," replied Bear with a smile.

CHAPTER 20

Early Saturday evening, Caleb, his hat pulled low, walked to the Café del Rio to meet B.R. for supper before going to the Menger hotel to meet with the investigator. He found B.R. already there, engrossed in conversation with the waitress, name of Topsannah, as he recalled.

Arriving at the table, Caleb pulled out a chair and the waitress turned away.

"I ordered for us both," said B.R., smiling.

"You seem in an uncommonly good mood," noted Caleb.

"Well, it's Saturday night and I hope to have a drink or three after we talk to the investigator."

"Hmm," responded Caleb. "I don't doubt that's all true, but I saw your face when I walked in."

"What are you saying? Talking in riddles and such."

"No use playing with me, B.R. I saw the way you was a looking at the waitress."

Smiling, B.R. said, "I ain't denying I find her attractive. Don't you?"

Caleb looked at his friend. "She's a purty thing, no doubt, but I'm thinking you were more than admiring her."

Suddenly leaning forward in his chair, B.R. said quietly, "Caleb, she's more than she appears. More than a pretty girl."

Caleb, chuckling quietly responded, "B.R., we saw a good many pretty girls in Mexico."

"I know, I know, but there is something about this one. I feel it. She's special."

Later, at the Menger hotel, B.R. and Caleb sat at a table with Clyde, dressed in his trademark gray suit, string tie and hat. They were both surprised at this small, slim, older man, as were most of his clients. He looked like a retired banker or lawyer, not a hard-nosed investigator.

"Please call me Clyde," said the man.

B.R. and Caleb introduced themselves and told the story. Clyde listened intently and asked dozens of questions, often about the smallest details.

"Sir, ah, aren't you going to write some of this down?" asked B.R.

"No, it's not necessary. I will remember," responded Clyde. "Frankly, Caleb, you don't strike me as unusual in appearance. It was dark. Why was the witness so sure it was you they saw?"

"Oh," said Caleb, lifting his hat a few inches so they Clyde could see his blond hair, and then setting it back on his head. "You see my fair hair? At the time, I wore it down to my shoulders."

"I see," replied Clyde.

"But the thing is," I didn't kill the girl.

Clyde and Caleb came to an agreement and made plans to meet again in a week, at the Menger, but on Sunday at noon.

Caleb and B.R. decided to visit a few out of the way saloons, on the lookout for a man with long blond hair. Clyde went to the sheriff's office and introduced himself. By luck, the Sheriff, having finished his supper, had stopped by the jail.

"What can I do for ya?" asked the Sheriff, spitting toward a can on the floor, but missing.

"Sheriff, I have been retained to investigate the murder of Lila Jennings of which Caleb Ford has been charged. His family, convinced of his innocence, have retained me."

"Why of course they are. What mother thinks her son is a cold-blooded killer?"

Holding his hat in his hand, Clyde shrugged his shoulders and said, "You are correct of course, but I must make a living and perhaps it will help the family to know for sure. May I ask the name of the witness?"

"I don't suppose the family mentioned his whereabouts?" asked the sheriff.

"They didn't know," replied Clyde, with a straight face.

The sheriff furnished Clyde with the name and address of the witness and Clyde retired to his room at the Menger hotel.

Caleb and B.R. visited several saloons, but didn't see a single person with blond hair of any kind.

As it grew late, Caleb said, "What say we stop by the Grand saloon just to have a look."

"I'm all done in partner, you good to go by your lonesome?"

"Sure, I'll meet you in the room," replied Caleb.

As he entered the saloon, Caleb looked around and saw Mollie sitting at a table with three young men, talking and smiling. He found an empty table and ordered a beer. He had already had several whiskeys and was feeling the effects. He sipped his warm beer and studied the men in the room, but didn't see anyone with long blond hair.

He was staring at his glass of beer when a hand brushed his neck and a voice said, "Mind if I join you, Cal from Austin?"

Caleb looked up to see Mollie taking the seat next to him. "Buy me a drink?"

Smiling, Caleb said, "Why sure."

Mollie waved at the bartender and smiled at Caleb.

After a moment of embarrassed silence, the two began to talk.

"I'm surprised to see you again," said Mollie, "but glad."

"Well, I'm happy to see you again," responded Caleb. "How have you been?"

Easy conversation followed, as Caleb, the whiskey and beer working on him, relaxed and enjoyed sitting and talking with this pretty young woman.

She listened intently, smiling and frowning, occasionally touching Caleb as he talked. She even asked a few questions to clarify what he said. They talked about the cold weather and she told him a funny story about a drunken cowboy. As they talked, he didn't even notice that he was on his third beer. He began to share some personal history as he talked.

He told her his fiancée had married another while he was away in the war, and finding farming a difficult business, he had drifted and found he enjoyed cowboying.

"You want another drink?" he asked.

"I don't really, and it's just tea you know, but if you want me to stay you'll have to buy another one." She smiled apologetically.

Shaking his head, he said, "I figured and I do." He lifted his hand and waved to the bartender and pointed at Mollie.

"I was married," said Mollie, quietly. "At age eighteen. My husband was killed in the war."

"I'm sorry," said Caleb. "It was a waste in many ways. So many young men dying on both sides. You'd a thought, well, you'd a thought the cruelty and wrongness of the evil institution would've been enough for folks to rally against it and end it without a war."

Mollie sat, sipped her tea and looked at him. "I know. Daddy said it was more to some folks, even those who were opposed to slavery, here in the south. He said they didn't like the federal government telling them what they could do and not do."

"Yes, I've heard that."

"As I recall, he also said here in Texas, only about a quarter of folks owned slaves."

"I didn't know. I hail from a free state, Ohio, but I've heard maybe half the white people in some of the southern states had slaves. It seems to me it was just so established; people were afraid to speak up." After a minute of silence, he sighed. "I better be getting on. I've had more than enough to drink. Maybe I'll see you again. If I don't, you take care. I enjoyed your company. And again, I'm sorry for mistaking, ah, what you do for a living."

She smiled a sad smile and in a second was up and away. As Caleb reached the door, he looked back to see her smiling and talking to another cowhand. Well, he thought, we all have to earn our living. With that, he was out the door and on his way to his room.

CHAPTER 21

After the auction, things moved quickly. Johnny found the sale agent, paid him and obtained the paperwork for the ownership of the horses. The man was professional, but seemed unhappy and nervous. When they had completed their business, he sent Johnny to see a man who helped him secure transport on a ship bound for Galveston leaving the next day. By early evening the horses had been moved and secured on the ship.

Johnny and Jameson felt good. Things were set and they would be headed home the next morning.

"What say we cross back over the river and have some supper?" said Johnny.

Jameson was eager to see the French Quarter, so after crossing back over the ferry, he and Johnny walked up toward it. They found the Café du Monde and marveled at both the coffee and the beignets. The mix of people, cultures and languages was fascinating, especially to Jameson. The two began to walk, taking in the city and found themselves on Bourbon street where they entered a saloon which offered ale. The two men were served by a very pretty girl and drank two glasses each and asked about a place they might find a decent meal.

"We would like to try some Creole food," explained Johnny to the bartender.

"Try Tujague's on Decatur."

"Much obliged," said Johnny.

Discovering it was nearly a mile to their destination, the two men decided to walk and see more of the city. Arriving at the restaurant, they ate a gumbo consisting of vegetables, fish and spicy seasoning.

"Rosalinda would marvel at this," commented Johnny, as he ate his bowl of gumbo with bread.

"It's different," was all Jameson had to say on the matter.

"Have you changed your mind about accompanying me back to Galveston on the ship?" asked Johnny.

Looking up from his bowl, Jameson looked at Johnny. "Being as how I didn't die on the way here, although I was sure I was going to, I reckon I will."

"Some have said you might not feel the effects after the first time."

"I pray they're right," replied Jameson.

Neither took notice of the two men who had followed them in and were now sitting across the room. Finishing their meal, Johnny and Jameson walked out onto the street and stopped to light smokes. The gas lamps mounted on posts a block apart had been lit and provided enough light to see to walk, although once a person got a short distance from the lamps, the light was non-existent. The two men who had followed them into the restaurant stepped outside and at the corner, stopped and rolled their own cigarettes, as they furtively kept an eye on Johnny and Jameson.

On the way back to their hotel, Johnny and Jameson stopped at a saloon and drank a whiskey each. Not long after they left, in the middle of a block, where it was dark, a young woman approached them and moving very close to Johnny, purred, "I have a room nearby handsome."

"Thank you no," said Johnny, stepping back, even as the woman pressed against him.

Taking the woman's arm, he tried to push her away, but she resisted. Finally, he took both of her arms and pushed her away from him, firmly, but not harshly. However, she suddenly tumbled backward and fell, then began to yell and curse him loudly.

Shocked, Johnny looked at her and then tried to help her up, but she flailed her arms and continued to curse. Stepping back as a few pedestrians stopped to watch the altercation, Johnny and Jameson quickly strove away.

"What the hell was that about?" asked Jameson.

"I've no idea," said Johnny, "but I suspect if we had stayed, a man would have appeared and demanded money."

"Of course," said Jameson. "Of course."

When Jameson and Johnny walked away, the two men following them and watching from the shadows, stepped out and greeted the woman.

"It worked," said one man to the other. "He'll believe the story and go quietly."

The other man handed the woman some money. "Go," he told her and, after putting the money in her dress, close to her bosom, she smiled and disappeared into the night.

Johnny and Jameson had only gone two blocks, when two Metropolitan Police, dressed in blue frocks and driving a wagon with a cage on it, pulled ahead of them, stopped, dismounted and approached them. Stepping to the sidewalk, the smaller policeman addressed Johnny.

"Sir, might we have a word?" he asked.

"What can I do for you?" asked Johnny, clearly surprised.

"I am afraid a young woman has made a complaint. She told us a man fitting your description assaulted and robbed her. I'm afraid you'll have to come to the station and see if she identifies you tomorrow. For now, you are under arrest," said the larger man. "Do you have any weapons on you?"

"I've a knife in my boot," said Johnny, his voice steely. "Might I ask the amount of my fine? Money is what you want I think."

"Don't make us add bribery to your problems," said the small policeman, as the larger one pulled Johnny's knife from his boot.

"He didn't do a thing," said Jameson. "I was right there. A lady of the night offered her services. He told her no, but she was insistent."

"You can come to court in the morning and bear witness," stated the smaller man, placing iron hand restraints on Johnny.

Thinking quickly, Johnny said, "Jameson, if there's a delay, take my gear from the hotel and get on that ship in the morning and tend to the horses. I'll send you a telegram with my plans to the Menger hotel in San Antonio. They know me there."

The policemen were leading Johnny to the back of the wagon, as Jameson, his voice strained, said, "Okay Johnny, the Menger you say?"

"Yes!" yelled Johnny, who was trying to lift himself up into the wagon with his hands chained together, as the big policeman shoved him in and slammed the door and placed a lock on it. Inside were two other men, both wearing restraints and judging from their appearance, very intoxicated.

Johnny couldn't figure out exactly what was happening. At first he thought the girl was a set-up, to get money from him somehow without actually robbing him, but now he didn't see how she hoped to gain. When the police said he was under arrest, he immediately assumed they had seen the girl fall down and were shaking him down for money, but they were taking him to jail.

As the wagon bumped down the brick lined road, Johnny decided that either the girl had really complained or more likely, the system was set up to arrest as many people as possible that dressed like they had some money. He would probably be given a chance to pay a hefty fine and avoid a trial. Damn the bad luck.

Finally, the wagon pulled up to a dark door on the side of the Parish Prison on Orleans and St. Ann. It was a huge, three-story stone building. The two policemen unlocked the cage door and removed the two drunks, before re-locking the door.

"We'll be back for you," said the smaller policeman.

The two men returned in a few minutes and helped Johnny down from the cage on the back of the wagon. The smaller policeman took his arm and began to lead him to the door, when suddenly, without warning, someone grabbed Johnny around the neck and pressed a sweet-tasting rag to his face.

Johnny reacted so violently, he, the man holding his arm and the one behind him all fell as a group, hitting the ground in a fierce struggle, but the man was able to hold the rag over Johnny's face as he bucked and struggled. A third man appeared and pressed his knee into Johnny's neck. Two men passed by, but seeing the police struggling with a man, they crossed the street and hurried on their way. Five minutes later, Johnny lay still. The cloth was removed, again soaked with chloroform and replaced over his nose and mouth; a small piece of rawhide used to tie it into place.

One of the three policemen waved his hand and a man driving a wagon rolled into sight and stopped by the police wagon. Johnny was thrown into the back of the wagon; a blanket was tossed over him and his hat, which had fallen off, was thrown in the wagon as the wagon rolled away with its cargo.

Jameson could not believe that Johnny had been arrested. Unsure of what to do, he walked back the way they had come in search of the woman, but couldn't find her. He asked where the jail was and was given directions to the Parish Prison.

"That'll be where you'll find him," a man told him.

He was almost arrested himself, right there in the jail. Jameson was getting red in the face and yelling his insistence that Johnny was there and he wanted to see him. The jail clerk insisted that no one named Johnny Black or fitting his description had been arrested that night.

"Damn it man, I was there when they took him into custody. I saw them put him in the wagon with the cage."

"The officers likely turned him loose. Happens sometimes," explained the clerk.

This gave Jameson hope, so he left and headed for the hotel. Arriving, he went up to Johnny's room and pounded on the door, but there was no answer. He went down and described Johnny to the desk clerk, but he said no one fitting that description had come in while he had been on duty and that was three hours now.

Jameson walked outside, built himself a cigarette, stood and smoked, thinking. This whole thing is wrong, he thought. It don't feel right. Finally, he decided he would do what Johnny had told him. Hopefully Johnny would be here in the morning or would meet him at the ship.

CHAPTER 22

Clyde was sitting at a kitchen table, a cup of coffee in front of him. On the other side of the table a man sat, a cup of coffee in front of him.

"If you can just tell me, in your own words, what you saw the night the young woman was killed, please," said Clyde.

"I've explained several times. To the sheriff, to the district attorney, to the grand jury."

"I understand sir, but if I could trouble you to explain once more."

Sighing, the man took a sip of his coffee, sat it back on the saucer and said, "I wouldn't have noticed anything. I was walking, it was late, two men walked by, I couldn't tell you a thing about them, as I wasn't interested or paying attention. But suddenly a fellow ran by, not far from me. The fact that he was running was what caught my notice."

"How far away was the man, the one running?" asked Clyde.

"Not ten feet, but his hat was pulled low. What caught my eye was his long blond hair. It was long, bouncing off his shoulders."

"Did he have a beard or mustache?" asked Clyde.

The man drank some more coffee and Clyde sipped his. There was silence. The man closed his eyes.

Opening his eyes, the man said, "No, he was clean shaven."

After a few more questions, Clyde thanked the man for his time and the coffee, replaced his hat on his head and bid the man a good day.

An hour later, Clyde was in the Grand saloon, talking to the bartender who told Clyde everything he knew about the dead girl, Lila Jennings and the night she was murdered.

"Did by any chance, Ms. Jennings have a dispute with any of the customers. Maybe one wanted more than talk and a dance and got upset at being denied." suggested Clyde.

Before the man could answer, Clyde placed a gold coin on the bar top. "For your time, but I need complete and honest answers. No more. No less."

"There's always a few, especially when they've had a few drinks, who get too friendly and we have to put 'em out."

Clyde looked at the man, but didn't speak.

The silence grew long, then the bartender said, "Well, now that I think about it, there was a fellow. Didn't cause no trouble, just the opposite. He would come late, not long afore closing and sit in the back and watch Lila. Two or three times a week. Haven't seen him since Lila died."

"Can you describe the man?" asked Clyde.

"Mid-thirties I'd guess. Dark hair and mustache."

One by one, Clyde interviewed the saloon girls that worked in the saloon. There were five of them and Clyde didn't find out much new until the very last one.

"She was in love," said the girl.

"I see," replied Clyde. "So, were you her friend?"

"Yes, we shared a room upstairs. We talked. She was so sweet."

"Who was she in love with?"

"James. He's married."

"Ah," said Clyde. "Did you tell anyone about James?"

The girl shook her head no, shrugged and replied, "No one asked."

"Did they ever quarrel, do you know?"

"They were in love. Really in love. I can't imagine them quarreling."

"Do you know where I can find James?"

She looked at him. "I don't want to cause him any trouble."

"I won't give away his secret to his wife," said Clyde.

"He lives with his wife over on Elm street in a green house, but he clerks for a lawyer. I don't know which one."

"Thank you, I'll be discreet," said Clyde.

There were a number of lawyers, but when Clyde walked in the door of the second one, he knew he had found James. The man matched the description given by the bartender.

"Could we have a word in private?" asked Clyde.

The conversation was short. The man confessed to being in love with Lila and meeting her several times a week in secret. They were making plans to run away together as soon as he finished reading law and was admitted to the bar.

"Did your wife know about Lila?" asked Clyde.

"She was suspicious. I was playing poker once a week with a group of friends and I would leave early to meet Lila. When I started going out two or three times a week, my wife was distressed. I had to see Lila, I had to, you see, but I don't think my wife knew for a fact that I was seeing anyone."

"Were you meeting Lila, the night she was killed?"

"No and that's why I don't understand why she was out that late. She should have gone to her room after work."

Clyde thanked the man, assured him his secret was safe and nodded goodbye.

Lila's friend at the saloon was working, so Clyde ordered a beer, and waved her over as he ordered a drink for her. She sat and looked at him, her face concerned and confused.

"Don't fret," said Clyde, "I just had another question and didn't want to interfere with your duties."

The girl, relieved, smiled.

"The night Lila died, was she meeting James? Do you know if that's why she left?"

"Well, she wasn't supposed to, they had certain nights, nights that James was supposed to be playing poker. But she got a note, saying he wanted to meet."

"Is the note in her room?"

"It might be. In her dresser."

"I'll have a word with the bartender if you don't mind taking a look."

A few minutes later, the girl came back down and joined Clyde at the bar, handing him a small folded paper.

"Thank you," said Clyde, touching his hat as he walked away.

CHAPTER 23

Jameson arose early and when no one answered his knock, he pressed a knife between the door and the door-jam to bypass the lock on Johnny's room. It was empty and the bed unslept in. He took Johnny's bag and rifle, grabbed his own gear and went straight to the Parish Prison. He listened in disbelief when a new clerk told him the same thing he had been told the night before. No one named Johnny Black or fitting that description had been arrested the night before. This was like a bad dream. After a quick breakfast, Jameson walked to the ship, his hopes rising, thinking, praying Johnny was waiting for him there, but his mood sank when he realized he wasn't.

Jameson boarded the ship and checked on the horses. The paperwork was in Johnny's bag and his mind was so focused on what had happened to Johnny, he didn't realize he wasn't sea sick as the ship churned its way on its forty-hour trip to Galveston.

Johnny awoke in pain, nauseated and confused. His head was hurting badly, it was pitch black and he didn't know where he was. Laying still, he breathed slowly, trying to collect his thoughts.

He moved one of his hands and realized he was lying on dirt. Although he was still wearing his greatcoat, he felt cold. He drew air in through his nose and the odor was of earth, dank, like a cellar. Was he in a cellar, he wondered? After listening for a few minutes and hearing nothing, he sat up and looked around. Darkness greeted him.

Slowly, his head cleared and the pounding pain in it lessened. He took an inventory. His pockets were empty, save for a small packet of cigarillos and four matches he had stuck in his coat pocket. Feeling around him in the dirt, he found his hat and put it on.

Pulling out a cigarillo, he struck a match, lit it and held the match out to look around. As best he could tell, he was in a cellar. As he held the match up, he saw the iron bars. He was very sore and sat and smoked while he gathered his thoughts. It came to him then, as his head cleared. The woman, the arrest by the police and the sweet-tasting rag; the struggle. He seemed to be in jail, but it was too quiet. As it occurred to him that he had been kidnapped; knocked out by either the use of chloroform or ether, two drugs used by the surgeons during the war when operating on wounded men, a chill convulsed through his body.

It was likely chloroform that was used to render him unconscious, he thought. It worked quicker. Thinking the situation over, he knew it had to be the work of the man at the auction. Peterson. The man everyone kept warning him about. It was the only thing that made sense. People did things for a reason, usually a monetary one, but often enough for emotional ones. Jealousy, anger, revenge. The fact that he wasn't killed and tossed in the river told him the man wanted him, Johnny, to know who was responsible. Well, if they didn't shoot him through the bars, he'd go down fighting.

He didn't fear death. In fact, he had made his peace with it during the Civil War. He was so sure he was going to be killed he accepted it. The only thing that distressed him was what his death would mean for Rosalinda and Lucrecia. He hadn't been a regular church goer for years. It wasn't that he didn't believe in a higher power, which he did. It seemed to him that the world was just too complex to not have a creator. He had been raised a Baptist, but had attended church with Rosalinda, a Catholic, from time to time. After considering for a minute, he said a prayer. Not for himself, but for those he cared about.

His head hurting, he stretched out on the dirt floor and slept.

Jameson didn't drink alcohol and ate little on the journey back to Galveston on the ship. His mood was dark and his mind racing with thoughts. Reaching Galveston, he made arrangements for himself and the horses to travel by train, first to Harrisburgh and then to Waelder. Having completed his business, he found a telegraph office and sent a dispatch to the Menger hotel inquiring about a message from Johnny Black and advising the hotel manager he would pay for a response when he returned to San Antonio.

It didn't take long for the return reply. No telegram or message from Mr. Black. Jameson felt sick. His hopes dashed. Picking up his and Johnny's rifles and travel bags, he walked to the train station.

The train trip was uneventful. All Jameson could think about was Johnny. Arriving at the Waelder train station, Jameson supervised the unloading of the horses and wrangled them to the stables where his horses and mud wagon were located. Returning to the train station, Jameson telegraphed again and waited for a reply. It was negative. No word from Johnny. With a sick feeling, he returned to the stables, recovered his mud wagon and horses and hired two men to help him with the trip home. After all the horses were fed and with the new horses on a lead, one man on the seat beside him holding a rifle, the other man sitting in the back of the mud wagon; Jameson started the final leg of his trip back to San Antonio.

CHAPTER 24

One week after hiring Clyde, B.R. was able to leave work just after the noon meal, having won a buck-off on the ranch and he found Caleb in his room, reading a dime novel called, *The Boy Spy.*

"Howdy," said B.R., entering the room.

"You get fired?" asked Caleb, "Or did you give notice?"

"Neither my amigo. You're looking at the man who rode Tornado to a stand-still."

"Tornado?"

"We was trying to saddle-break that fool horse for a week. He's throwed every wrangler on the place at least twice. Some fellows refused to get on him again. I finally rode him down to a walk and the foreman gave me the afternoon off."

"Well how about that," said Caleb.

"How you finding that book?" asked B.R.

"Pretty exciting, but I'm going crazy cooped up in this room. I was sleeping during the day and walking around at night, just to be outside. Have you heard from Mr. Clyde?"

"No, I stopped by the Menger, but he weren't in and there was no message for me."

Signing, Caleb said, "At five dollars a day, I hope he's making progress."

B.R. grinned. "I'm thinking to have my supper at Café del Rio. You interested?"

"It's clear you don't realize that waitress you favor has eyes for me or you wouldn't be inviting me along."

"Caleb, you're a little balled-up. It ain't she's got eyes for you; she just feels sorry for your ugly self."

His face serious, Caleb replied, "B.R., I hope you've thought this out."

Looking away and silent for a moment, B.R. replied to the wall, "I can't explain it, truth be told. I'm drawn to the woman and can't help thinking about her."

The two men smoked and napped until evening when B.R. left to have his supper. The two agreed to meet at the Alamo at eight that evening.

Topsannah showed no sign of even recognizing B.R. when he came in. She waited on him politely, him grinning the entire time, her face impassive. When she brought his meal to his table, B.R. tried to make conversation with her, but her answers were short and finally she said, "I have tables to see to."

He left that evening feeling as though things were going backward in his endeavor to befriend Topsannah. Women, he thought. There's just no way to figure 'em out.

Caleb and B.R. met at the Alamo at eight and began to make the rounds of saloons, having one beer at each one, looking for a man with long blond hair. They visited four and B.R. took to telling the bartenders he was looking for a friend, describing him as having 'long blond hair', but they came up empty. As they left the last one, Caleb said, "I reckon we'll have to hope the investigator comes up with something. You want to stop by the Grand?"

"You're going back to the scene of the crime again?" asked B.R.

"Oh, nobody recognizes me there, and well, there's a girl there I kinda like talking to."

"Caleb, you're willing to risk getting caught and hung, to talk to a girl? When you was robbed that knock on the head must have rid you of what little smarts them bucking horses ain't rid you of."

Caleb looked at B.R. "You're right. It don't make no sense, but I reckon I'm going."

B.R. grinned. "Well, nobody ever accused me or you of being smart. Any no how, if you're going to talk to a girl, I think I might stop by the Café del Rio. They ought to be closing up soon. Maybe I can walk Topsannah home."

Caleb and B.R. both laughed and with a nod, turned to go their separate ways. B.R. stopped and yelled at Caleb, "If I don't see you in the room, remember, we're to meet Mr. Clyde tomorrow at noon for an update."

Smiling, Caleb waved and strove away as B.R. headed for the Café del Rio. B.R. was able to get in the door, but was told by Topsannah's father-n-law that the café was closed.

"I thought I'd see if I could walk Ms. Topsannah home," explained B.R.

The man stared at him, then said, "I will tell her you are here."

B.R. waited for a full two minutes before he came back out the door to the kitchen. "She says she has work to do, but thank you anyway."

Disappointed, B.R. touched his hat, said, "Gracias, buenas noches," and stepped out in the night. Standing outside the café, he built himself a quirly, smoked for a few minutes, thinking about having a few more drinks, but decided he'd just as well head for Caleb's room and turn in.

As he passed a noisy saloon, three men, all drunk, stepped out, almost colliding with him, but he took no notice of them. He was so engrossed in his thoughts of Topsannah, he wasn't paying attention to anything and didn't see the startled expressions on their faces as they recognized him. The three stood for a moment, passing around a bottle of whiskey they had brought out of the saloon. After a quick discussion, the three followed after him down the dark street.

Two blocks down the street, Reginald, the leader of the group and the man who B.R. had fought in the Café del Rio in defense of Topsannah, stepped up behind B.R. and slammed the empty whiskey bottle against the side of his head. A sound emitted from B.R., even as things began to get blurry, his knees buckled and he fell in a heap. The three men began to kick his prone body as they laughed. B.R. was conscious, but disorientated as he tried to cover his head and curl up to protect himself. Once, he tried to crawl forward, but stretching opened his body to his attacker's kicks and he quickly rolled back into a ball.

The three men, somewhat exhausted by their efforts, stopped momentarily and stood staring at the broken heap on the ground. Blood was flowing over B.R.'s face from several places above his eyes where the attacker's boots had landed and split the skin. It was also pouring from his head, where the bottle had struck him.

"I want this cowpuncher to know who whupped him," said Reginald, drawing back his leg to kick B.R. in the head again.

Once, when he was a teenager, Reginald's mother had brought home a cat. Reginald had pulled the cat's tail as hard as he could one day and to his shock, the cat had flung itself at him, clawing, scratching and biting him. It felt like forever before he could disengage himself from the infuriated cat. His experience with the cat came to him in his dreams sometimes and to his horror, he thought he was experiencing it again as something landed on his back and began to claw, scratch and bite him about his face and neck.

Reginald screamed! He twisted and tried to grab the thing on his back. "Help me!" he screamed at his two friends whose eyes were wide as they saw what appeared to be an aberration from hell, appearing suddenly out of the darkness and leaping onto Reginald's back.

One of the men turned and ran. The other stood motionless, his mouth agape, watching Reginald flail his arms and run in a circle as he screamed. B.R.'s head cleared and he rolled over and struggled to his feet. Just as he did, Reginald threw Topsannah from his back. She landed on her back, the wind gushing out of her in a 'whoosh'.

Turning, Reginald lifted his foot to stomp her face, when B.R. took a step and launched himself into Reginald, both of them landing a few feet away rolling as one. When they stopped, both struggled to their feet and both were terrifying sights. Reginald's face was a mass of bleeding scratches, one ear was hanging from his head, having been nearly been bitten off and was dripping blood. His normally neatly brushed hair looked like a pile of wind-blown brush and his shirt was ripped. Wild eyed he looked at his friend, still standing still, as if frozen in place.

"Get him!" screamed Reginald. "Now!"

Some three feet from Reginald, B.R. wiped blood from his eyes with his sleeve and, taking five or six steps, reached Topsannah.

"Are you hurt?" he asked, his voice full of concern.

"Estoy bien," she said firmly, rising to her feet, having regained her breath.

B.R.'s face broke into a smile, a contrast to his bloody, battered face. "Yo Tambien," he said, quietly, before turning to look at Reginald.

"Hello Reginald," said B.R. "We meet again."

Reginald stared at B.R. and looked at his friend who was still standing with his mouth open, in a state of shock, as B.R. advanced toward him.

"Get away from me!" screamed Reginald, who began to backup.

Silent, B.R. kept walking, his hands at his sides, but at the moment he was within arm's reach of Reginald he lifted his left hand, faked a jab and hit Reginald square in the face with a jolting right cross. He was prepared to continue the assault, but Reginald had stepped back and crumbled to the ground, unconscious. When B.R. turned to face the other man, he saw him running into the night. Weakness suddenly flooded B.R. and he staggered. Suddenly, Topsannah was there, her arm around him.

"I know doctor," she said. "Mexican doctor."

B.R. nodded and the two stumbled away.

While B.R. was being treated by the doctor, Caleb was sitting in the Grand Saloon, talking to Mollie and thoroughly enjoying himself.

"Mollie, I told you how I gave up farming and took up cowboying, drifting as it were. It ain't forever, mind you. I want my own ranch someday and kids, lots of kids."

She smiled and her face softened. "I want a family also Caleb. Folks judge me of course, being a saloon girl and all, but I don't do anything sinful. Some men wouldn't want to marry me, knowing I'm a saloon girl, but I'm young and making more money than I could at anything else."

"I'd marry you," exclaimed Caleb, grinning.

"Hush that foolish talk," responded Mollie, laughing.

"There's a dance next Saturday night. Would you like to go?"

Smiling, Mollie said, "I'd love to, but I have to work. If I don't come on a Saturday Ed would fire me."

"Okay then, how about we take a ride, have a picnic on Sunday afternoon?"

Mollie sat, looking at him. "I don't think I better, Cal."

"Why not?" asked Caleb, hurt feelings in his face.

Standing up, Mollie said, "It's late," kissed him on the cheek and disappeared in the crowd.

Mollie's kiss sent Caleb's spirits soaring.

CHAPTER 25

Caleb was up and shaven when B.R. finally rolled out of his bed in Caleb's rented room. It took several minutes before Caleb actually noticed B.R.'s swollen, black and blue face. Stitches stretched for several inches above both eyes; one eye was swollen shut, his lips were swollen and the side of his head shaven, where more stitches protruded. Yet, B.R. was grinning from ear to ear.

"Morning Caleb," he said. "How are you this fine morning?"

Caleb stared at B.R., astonished at his appearance. "What happened?"

"Topsannah saved my life," replied B.R., taking his trousers from the back of a chair and pulling them on. "You should have seen her. She was a wildcat. I don't think the woman knows what fear is."

"What happened?" repeated Caleb, still in a state of shock at B.R.'s appearance.

Wincing in pain as he pulled his boots on, B.R. said, "I'll tell you over breakfast. I need some coffee."

An hour later, breakfast finished and fresh coffee in front of them, B.R. and Caleb sat at the table, looking at each other. "You look like some kind of crazy man. Your face and head all messed up, your lips swollen and that dumb grin on your face. Did you see our waitress? I thought she was going to run when she saw you."

"Well, enough about me. Did you get to talk to that saloon girl you fancy?"

Sipping his coffee, Caleb, trying not to smile, said, "I did."

B.R. stared at Caleb and tilted his head.

"Now just a doggone minute. You've been holding back on me. Don't tell me you're falling for her?

An alarmed expression on his face, Caleb said, "No, no. I just like talking to her is all."

"What's her name?"

"Mollie."

"Amigo, for a fellow who didn't speak twenty words a day for the last year, it just seems a little odd that you got the sudden urge to talk."

Irritated, Caleb retorted, "Maybe she's a better listener than you."

"I swear, you're in love."

"Dang you B.R., if you wasn't already busted up I'd have you eating dirt."

Laughing, B.R. replied, "It appears I've hit on a tender spot."

"I don't want to talk about it. Let's go over to the stable where I left the appaloosa. I need to check on him and pay the owner for another week of board. You bring some of the money I gave you to hold?"

"I did. I'm thinking Mr. Clyde might ask for some when we see him today."

The two friends arrived at the Menger hotel a few minutes before noon and stood in the lobby, waiting on Clyde. Seeing B.R.'s face, guests would veer away, but try to get a second look. As the clock struck noon, Clyde and another man entered the hotel and seeing Caleb and B.R. approached them. Clyde took no notice of the damage to B.R.'s face and head.

As the men shook hands, Clyde said, "Caleb, I don't know if you remember your attorney, Mr. Clack."

"Oh, yes sir. Our meeting was brief, but I remember. Howdy."

"I have some news and took the liberty of bringing your attorney along. Why don't we take a table in the restaurant?"

A few minutes later, sitting at a table and sipping coffee, Caleb was nervous. The fact that Clyde had brought along Caleb's lawyer concerned him. Maybe, he thought, they were going to encourage him to turn himself in.

"Caleb, there have been developments in your case. I have been working with the district attorney for the last few days and based on some information I discovered, the district attorney has arrested a woman for the murder for which you were indicted."

Caleb sat. He couldn't get his mind to work. Was he in the clear?

B.R. started to speak, but Clyde held up his hand. "Ms. Jennings was meeting regularly with a married man. His wife discovered the affair and sent Lila a note, which Lila thought was from her lover. When they met, the woman, dressed in her husband's clothing, killed her. When she ran, her long blond hair, which she had tucked up under a man's hat, fell out and was seen by the witness."

"A woman. Who'd a thought," said B.R.

"Caleb, there are wanted posters out offering a reward for your capture. Here is the paperwork declaring you free of all charges," said the attorney, handing Caleb some folded papers. "I'd keep them close."

Caleb, feeling as though he were dreaming, took the papers.

"Ah, what about the escape?" asked B.R., looking over at Caleb, who still hadn't spoken.

The attorney smiled. "The district attorney has dropped those charges. Being as how you are innocent; it didn't take much convincing."

"So that's it?" asked B.R., speaking for Caleb.

"There is the matter of my fee," responded Clyde with a smile.

"I also require an additional payment for my time in dealing with the final results," replied the attorney.

Caleb smiled. "Gentlemen, best money I ever spent."

CHAPTER 26

Something woke Johnny up. He lay in the dark listening. What was it? A rat maybe. He listened, and there, he heard it. A low moaning sound.

A few minutes later, as the sun rose, some light found itself into the building through small cracks in the high roof, where Johnny was imprisoned, and he studied his surroundings. He was in a small, windowless, one-room building; solid timber walls all around. Iron bars in front of him and on one side, dividing the room into two cells. What appeared to be a door covered by iron bars could be seen in the wall, about four feet from the bars that enclosed his cell.

In the cell next to him, he could see a dark form. As he was studying it, it moved.

"Good morning," said a voice, emanating from the dark shape.

"Morning," said Johnny, his voice sounding strange to him.

"I'm George," said the man.

"Johnny."

"Why, you're a white man," said George in surprise.

"Yes," said Johnny. "By any chance do you know where we are?"

"I sure do. We're the guests of Lord Peterson, owner of the Peterson Sugar Plantation and Processing Plant and proud owner of nearly one hundred slaves."

"Slavery was outlawed in this country some nine years ago," replied Johnny.

Suddenly he could see brilliant white teeth in the darkness as George smiled.

"Yes sir, I heard that, but you see that don't apply in the Kingdom of Peterson."

"What are you saying?" asked Johnny.

"I'm saying as far as Mr. Peterson and his henchmen are concerned, slavery is still a fact."

"How is that possible?"

George let out a loud sigh. "Mr. Johnny, we on a two thousand-acre plantation. Mr. Peterson is very rich and powerful. I was a servant in the house for a while. The sheriff dines here regular, course he doesn't know what's going on. He thinks Mr. Peterson a fine man. One time, some federal troops came in and Mr. Peterson, well, he liked to be called Lord Peterson, he showed them around. They talked to some workers, black folks. They all said what they had been told to say. They happy, they free, they getting paid for working for Mr. Peterson."

"But why?" asked Johnny.

"Ha. You don't sound like no fool. Why you think? They scared. We all scared. Some folks think it was a trick, to test them."

Johnny tried to think. The very idea shocked him.

"What brings you here any no how?" asked George.

"I reckon I made Peterson mad," said Johnny.

"Yep, I made him mad myself. I stole a horse and left. Didn't get far before they found me. Anyways, you ain't the first white man made him mad. There's more than one buried under the cane." He was quiet for a moment, then continued, "There should be a chamber pot in the corner and a canteen of water; probable been there a while. Oh, you'll likely find a little straw in the corner. Jackson, he the foreman, he's the meanest man I ever met, likes to hurt people. He whupped up on me pretty good. I got here two days ago and be here for another day with no food. Then I'll likely get the whip, but probably no more than twenty lashes. I a good worker and they not want to keep me down for too long."

Jameson and the two men he had hired arrived in San Antonio tired, dusty, hungry and thirsty. It was three days after Christmas. The only good thing about the trip was there had been no trouble. The horses were all in good shape and for that, Jameson was thankful.

Jameson explained to Ellison, the stable owner, what had happened and learning that Johnny Black, a legend in this part of the country was missing, Ellison was shocked. When all the stock had been brushed, fed and watered, Jameson and his two men walked to a restaurant and ate. Afterward, he paid them off, added enough for stagecoach fare back to Waelder and returned to the stables. He badly wanted a drink, but he felt an urgent need to report Johnny's disappearance to his wife, although he dreaded it as he had nothing before. He asked Ellison if he knew how to get to the Black homestead.

"I've never been out there, but Mr. Black has been here many times and as much we've talked, I have an idea of where his place is. You can ask, you get out in Medina county. The thing is, it'll be dark afore you get there and the horses could use some rest."

"You're right. I need to check at the Menger hotel, see if there's been a message. Either way, I'll spend the night, see you at daybreak."

There was no message from Johnny and after a restless night, Jameson had breakfast and returned to the stables. He found the Black homestead with only one stop for directions and turned off the main road toward the house. Rosalinda saw the wagon from the kitchen window and thinking Johnny had returned at last, wiped her hands and hurried to the door.

They had decided to wait on the Christmas celebration until Johnny returned. He had planned to be back for Christmas, but travel was uncertain and now, here he was. Her heart leaped.

Standing on the porch, she watched as Jameson drove his mud wagon into the yard and up to the barn. Besides the four horses pulling his wagon, he had four horses, two of them very tall, on leads, trailing the wagon. So, she thought, Johnny had bought his Percherons. How thrilled he must be. Oddly, she didn't see him. He must be following the wagon. Perhaps he had been delayed in town. She walked out to the barn and greeted Jameson.

"Good morning sir!" she exclaimed, a smile on her face.

The bearded, older man who looked at her and then removing his hat, and looking at the ground, caused her body to flush with anxiety. It was the man's expression, as though he had bad news. Henry Bear came out of the barn and approached, removing his gloves to shake hands, a smile on his face.

"Mrs. Black?" inquired Jameson, not noticing Henry approaching.

"Yes," she replied.

"My name's Jameson. I accompanied your husband, Mr. Black, to New Orleans to buy these horses," he said, waving his arm at the two Percherons and the two Morgans at the back of his wagon. "It was raining when he set out and figuring the stages wouldn't be running, he hired me to take him to meet the train in Waelder in my wagon and ah, I ended up going all the way with him."

Now, Rosalinda and Henry Bear were standing and looking at the man as though he were talking a foreign language.

"Well, the thing is, Mr. Black, Johnny that is, well, he's missing."

Thirty seconds of silence filled the air before Rosalinda said, "Why don't you come in Mr. Jameson and have some coffee and tell us what's happened. Henry, can the boys tend to the horses and you come in also?"

"Yes ma'am, I'll be there as quick as I task the lads."

Rosalinda introduced Jameson to her mother and father as well as Lucrecia.

"Johnny's missing, and Mr. Jameson is here to tell us what has happened. We'll just wait on Henry," she said, her voice calm, devoid of emotion.

"What the hell!" exclaimed Lupe, looking at Jameson with suspicion.

"Dios misericordioso," exclaimed Margarita.

A few minutes later, Rosalinda, her father, her mother, Henry and Jameson sat at the kitchen table. Everyone had coffee, but no one was drinking it except Jameson. All eyes were on him as he explained what had happened. He didn't tell them about the trouble on the road to Waelder or his sea sickness, but he did tell them about Peterson, the girl and Johnny's arrest. He finished by telling them Johnny had yelled at him to get on the boat with the horses and that he would telegraph the Menger hotel.

When he had finished, no one spoke. All sat, thinking their private thoughts and fears. Rosalinda almost broke into tears, but she didn't. Taking a deep breath, she said, "We must make a plan to find him. He is not dead."

Chapter 27

Johnny had been imprisoned for two weeks. His dark beard was full and he had lost weight. There was no heat, but the heavy walls and his great-coat kept him from freezing to death. George had been removed after a few days by a white man. The only other person he had seen was an older black man who came in once a day, to empty his chamber pot and bring him a tin plate of food, but no spoon. The food was always the same. Cornbread and salt pork. Once, he found a sweet potato on his plate and he was grateful. Every other day, he exchanged his canteen of water. He had tried to talk to the man, but was ignored. One day, when the door opened, he saw a white man with a whip and a shotgun standing outside the door when the black man entered.

He had one match and one cigarillo left. Strangely, he fretted more about that than the lack of food. The last time the old man had come, he had asked for tobacco and a spoon, but as usual, the man didn't speak.

Johnny had kept busy. George had been right about the hay. Just enough for a bed of sorts and an old blanket, filthy and full of holes lay in the corner. A few days after George was taken away, he realized the place ran on a schedule and, pulling the straw into a pile, he began to claw at the dirt floor, using the tin plate and his fingers, carefully spreading the dirt he removed over the other parts of the floor and then stretching the blanket over the hole and covering it with hay. Of course no one, but the elderly black man had been inside, but he continued. He had scratched a hole as big as his arm, three feet down, before he found the bottom of the logs. Tonight he would start enlarging the hole, but it was very slow work.

When the old man came, Johnny passed him his chamber pot, his plate and his canteen. The old man pushed the new tin of food and a canteen of water through a slot in the bottom of the flat, iron bars. He went outside to empty the pot and returned, passing it through the bars. Then, he dropped a small cloth sack into the cell, turned and left. In the sack, Johnny found a plug of chewing tobacco and a spoon. He smiled.

That evening, he decided to smoke his last cigarillo. As he sat and smoked, he wondered why Peterson hadn't been out to taunt him. It was likely the man was traveling. That or he wanted to let Johnny sit and suffer awhile. He only hoped Jameson had made it back and told Rosalinda. She was a smart woman and knowing her, would likely hire someone to come looking for him. If they killed him, which he was pretty sure was the ultimate plan, he hoped they would throw his body some place where it would be found.

Back at the homestead, Rosalinda had just announced the need for a plan, when there was a knock at the door. Startled, her nerves tight, she jumped. Then, forcing herself to relax, she said, "Excuse me," and answered it.

The doctor stood on the porch, hat in hand, in spite of the cold, his face strained. "Rosalinda," he said, when she opened the door.

"Oh, doctor, it's you. Come in."

"I can tell by your face; the news is true."

She looked at him.

"Ellison, at the stables, told someone, and well, word spread fast."

Coffee cups were refilled, a cup was found for the doctor and Rosalinda said, "Someone must go to New Orleans and look for him. We can't just sit and wait to hear from him or, well, hear that he's dead."

"He disappeared in New Orleans you say?" asked the doctor.

"Yes," said Jameson and gave the doctor a brief account.

"Not long ago I, ah, had an issue and hired a private investigator that Johnny recommended. The man is very good. I suggest we hire him to go to New Orleans to investigate."

There was some general discussion before Rosalinda said, "I am going. Mother can you see to Lucrecia for me? Henry can see to the homestead."

Her mother started to protest, thought better of it and nodded.

Henry said, "I'd like to accompany you ma'am. It'll be dangerous, a woman traveling that far."

The doctor studied Henry. "How are you feeling?"

Henry still had a good bit of pain in his hand where the snake had bitten him and his arm lacked the strength it once had, but he wasn't going to mention it. "I'm fine," said Henry.

"My foreman can look after our place and I will stay here with momma to see to your place," said Lupe. "The mares will foal in the next few weeks and I'm the most experienced."

"I'm going for sure," said Jameson.

Everyone's eagerness to help overwhelmed Rosalinda and she began to cry.

The doctor left to return to San Antonio and telegraph Clyde in Austin where Dependable Investigations was located. He would return the following day or as soon as he heard back. It was agreed he would ask at the telegraph office if any messages had come from Johnny or for Jameson.

It was agreed Jameson would spend the night, staying in Henry's old room in the barn.

Lupe left for his homestead to issue orders to his foreman, with plans to return the following day. Rosalinda began to pack for the trip to New Orleans.

Clyde had checked out of the Menger hotel, and was waiting at the stage line office for the stage to Austin, due in a couple of hours, although it was often late, when the boy came with a telegram. The boy had been to the Menger and the desk clerk and told him he might catch Clyde if he hurried. Clyde took the message, tipped the boy and tore it open. It was from his office clerk. The doctor he had worked for in San Antonio involving a fraud scheme, what a year ago, was trying to contact him about an emergency case. The doctor had telegraphed the office and said he would wait for a reply.

The telegraph operator, receiving the return telegraph, not for the doctor, but for Clyde, was confused, but decided it best to not say anything, but rather to carry out his duties. He sent one of his delivery boys with the message to the Menger.

Refolding the message and sliding it into his coat pocket, Clyde turned and walked to the telegraph office where he found the doctor, who was more than surprised when Clyde stepped into the office. In fact, the doctor found himself unable to speak for several seconds.

Clyde smiled, an unusual event for him, but he found some humor in the doctor's shock.

"You wanted to discuss an investigation with me?" asked Clyde calmly. Seeing the doctor's confusion, he continued, "I was in San Antonio on another matter which I have just concluded. My clerk telegraphed me at the hotel where I was staying and they sent your message to me at the stagecoach office where I was waiting for the stage back to Austin."

The doctor, frowning, looked at the telegraph operator who was keeping his head down in the pretense of studying a message. Turning back to Clyde he said, "Yes, yes, we need your help. Johnny Black has gone missing."

CHAPTER 28

B.R. and Caleb stood in front of John Christie's desk watching him read the papers the lawyer had given Caleb, declaring him free of all charges related to the murder of Lila Jennings.

Looking up, Christie said, "Welcome aboard, see the foreman." With that, he went back to his own paperwork.

When B.R. introduced Caleb to the foreman, the foreman stood looking at B.R.'s face and head. "I'm guessing you lost," he said dryly.

Smiling, Caleb offered, "Oh yes sir, he did, but a girl saved him."

"That a fact," said the foreman, interested. "Must be some girl."

Much to his displeasure, due to his injuries, B.R. was assigned to help the cook while Caleb was sent to work with the cowboys breaking a string of horses purchased from a ranch in Mexico. That evening, Caleb was almost knocked down and run over by his own horse, Champion, who, upon seeing him, broke into a dead run. It was a happy reunion; cowboy and horse.

The week was passing slowly for Caleb and B.R. who were both in a hurry for Saturday to come so they could ride into San Antonio and see Topsannah and Mollie. Friday, while trying to saddle-break a stallion, Caleb was tossed off and into the top rain of the fence. One leg hit the fence and then he went over, landing awkwardly. When he tried to get up, it felt like he had been shot all over again in his hip; the site of the old wound sent a stabbing pain through him and he collapsed. The other wranglers carried him out of the corral and to his bed in the bunkhouse and sent for the cook, who set bones and administered to other injuries.

Caleb winced and gritted his teeth as the cook poked and prodded. Finally, he announced Caleb had to be taken to town to see the doctor.

A wagon was fetched and Billy Ray, anxious to get away from kitchen duty offered to drive the wagon.

The cook looked at B.R. "There are potatoes need peeling," he said, "but seeing as how it's your friend, go ahead. Make sure you're here to help with breakfast."

As the wagon bounced along and Caleb groaned with pain, B.R. said, "A bit of good fortune, that stallion throwing you into the fence."

"The hell you say," replied Caleb, gritting his teeth.

"You don't have to act like that. I admit the good fortune is mainly mine. I hate peeling potatoes and cleaning pots and the like. We can eat supper at Café del Rio."

Caleb groaned in pain.

"Besides, I figured you was half-way carrying on so we could go to town. You are, ain't ya?"

Caleb's eyes narrowed as he gave B.R. a 'go to the devil look', but didn't answer.

The two stopped at the doctor's office, but found the office locked and no information about when he might return.

"Well, what say I take you to the Mexican doctor that patched me up?" asked B.R. "I think he speaks some English."

"It don't matter, I'm a hurting bad, B.R."

B.R. took two wrong turns, but finally found the doctor's office. B.R. helped Caleb into the office and onto a table. The doctor, a man in his thirties, said, "Hola, I am Doctor Hernandez."

Caleb nodded and the doctor began to examine him.

"Your hip is out of joint," said the doctor. "I can try to force it back into place, but it is very painful, so better we put you to sleep."

"Good, good," responded Caleb, "whatever you need to do."

"I don't have an ether or chloroform; I will have to send for some."

"How long does it take to push it back in?" asked Caleb, his face twisted in pain.

Shrugging, the doctor replied, "Maybe very quick. Maybe not."

"Then just do it, please."

The doctor walked away and returned with a leather strap. "So you don't bite your tongue in two."

Looking at B.R., who was realizing how badly Caleb was hurting, the doctor said, "Get a good hold of his shoulders."

Caleb screamed, bit down hard on the leather strap, gasped and passed out from the pain. When he awoke, a few minutes later, he saw the doctor and B.R. staring at him, and he was hurting, but the intense pain was gone.

"I feel better," said Caleb. The doctor smiled. B.R. laughed a nervous laugh.

"If there is no damage to you inside and if it doesn't come out again, I think you'll be able to walk and ride again in a month or two."

Using a wooden crutch and leaning on B.R., Caleb worked his way back out to the wagon and the doctor and B.R. helped him into the seat. The doctor handed him a bottle of laudanum. A few drops when the pain is bad," said the doctor. "If it comes out again, or if your skin has black or purple areas, you must see your doctor."

Smiling, Caleb said, "I reckon you're my doctor."

B.R. walked the horses, to keep the wagon from jolting. Arriving at the Café del Rio, B.R. helped Caleb down, handed him his crutch and the two entered the café and found a table.

"I'm a guessing if Mr. Christie don't fire you outright, you're gonna be in the kitchen helping me peel potatoes," said B.R., gleefully.

Caleb was about to reply when Topsannah appeared. Unsmiling, she placed coffee cups in front of them and filled them from a pot.

"Hola, Topsannah," said a smiling B.R.

"What would you have?" she asked, unsmiling.

"I wanted to thank you again for saving my life," said B.R. "It was a brave thing you done."

Topsannah looked at him. "Not to mention," she said.

Surprised at Topsannah's seemingly unconcerned attitude about the fight and visit to the doctor, B.R. ordered for both of them. Topsannah turned and walked away.

Sweating from pain, Caleb pulled the bottle of laudanum from his pocket and dripped a few rust-colored drops into his coffee.

"She seem mad to you?" asked B.R.

"Not particularly," replied Caleb, closing his eyes with the pain. "But you know, she doesn't strike me as the cheerful, talkative type."

Topsannah returned with plates of Machacas; tortillas wrapped around pork, eggs, potatoes and spices; a food both men had enjoyed while working in Mexico. Leaving the table without a word, she returned with a bowl of guacamole and the coffee pot.

As he ate, B.R. said, "They put corn in 'em here," and Caleb nodded, focused on his pain.

By the time the two men had finished eating and ordered pie and more coffee, Caleb was feeling the effects of the laudanum and had relaxed.

Looking at Caleb as he ate his pie, B.R. said, "You seem a right bit better. What's in them drops anyway? Do you know?"

"Yes," replied Caleb. "I was wounded in the war, spent some time in the hospital. I'm not sure what all is in it, but I know it's part Chinese opium and wine."

"I'd be careful amigo. Remember that woman we run across was addicted to opium?"

"I do," replied Caleb. "In that saloon in south Texas. The barkeep said she used to be a lady. She looked really old, but he said she claimed she had only just turned thirty."

The two sat and ate, sipped their coffee, lost in thought.

"What say we stop by the Grand and I'll introduce you to Mollie?" asked Caleb.

"I don't reckon you ought be drinking while you're taking that there medicine."

"No, I won't drink, but I'd like to see her."

"All right then," said B.R., looking around and waving at Topsannah.

When she arrived at their table, B.R. tried his best smile on her, but she stared at him solemnly. "We wanted to pay up, we got to get on."

B.R. paid and said, "Thank you again for saving my bacon."

Topsannah nodded and walked away to check on another table of customers.

After B.R. had helped Caleb outside and into the wagon, Caleb said, quietly, "Billy Ray, I don't want to throw water on your fire, but I don't reckon that girl has feelings for you."

B.R. looked over at Caleb. "I'm a starting to get that idea myself, but I reckon I'll give it another go or two afore I call it quits."

"You always was one for punishment," said Caleb. "Remember that time; you was throwed, what, ten, eleven times by that big roan? You just kept climbing back on."

B.R. laughed at the memory. "I could barely get out of the bunk the next day," he replied.

Arriving at the Grand Saloon, B.R. and Caleb found a table in the back and B.R. went to the bar to get a beer for himself and a coffee for Caleb. Being a Friday night, the place was beginning to get crowded.

B.R. drew some looks, his face swollen, the area around both eyes a mixture of colors; black, purple, green and yellow. The stitches above both eyes still protruding, although his hat covered his head wound.

Returning to the table, B.R. set Caleb's coffee in front of him, flopped into a chair and took a sip of his beer. As he started to speak to Caleb, he saw he was staring across the room, his face drawn.

Turning in his chair, B.R. saw a pretty girl at a table, sitting in the lap of a man, smiling and laughing. Two other men sat at the table. A bottle of whiskey sat in the center of the table.

B.R. knew at once this girl must be Mollie. "She's just doing her job," he said quietly to Caleb.

Still staring at her, Caleb said, "While you were at the bar, we looked at each other. She turned her head and kissed the man. The one whose lap she's sitting in."

B.R. sipped his beer.

Caleb stared at Mollie, his coffee sitting and growing cold. Finally, Caleb said, "What say we get on back. I notice you're the first to roll out now you're on kitchen duty."

Both men were silent on the trip home. B.R. helped Caleb to his bunk and found the foreman out back of the bunkhouse, smoking. He told him about Caleb and that the doctor said he'd be laid up a month or so, stretching the truth just a little.

"I figured his leg was broke," said the foreman. "Mr. Christie said find him a stool and let him help you in the kitchen."

B.R. let out a sigh of relief. "Yes sir," he said, and headed back in the bunkhouse to give Caleb the good news.

The next day, a Saturday, January 2, 1875, Mr. Christie paid all the hands. He had waited to pay them until the New Year as he didn't want them drinking and gambling away a month's wages on New Year's Eve. Everyone except Caleb and B.R. left for town to make up for missing the New Year celebrations. The two sat at a table, alone, playing conquian, a card game they had learned in Mexico. They had discussed going to town, but neither had the heart for it. They had a half-bottle of whiskey that B.R. had bought off another cowboy. He splashed some in their empty coffee cups. Caleb added a few drops of laudanum to his and the two played; most of the time in silence. Both considering the mysteries of women, love and life.

CHAPTER 29

Johnny was sleeping during the day and digging with the spoon at night. Just before daybreak, he would bury the spoon and the small bag of chewing tobacco. If he was taken from the cell, he didn't want Peterson's men to find them.

The spoon made all the difference. He was making good progress in enlarging the hole. It was so big now, he had to pile dirt on the corners of the old blanket to hold it in place over the hole. Noticing the cracks in the roof and wall beginning to show signs of light, he covered the hole and buried the spoon and tobacco. A short time later, he heard the door rattle as the lock was removed. It was earlier than usual, he thought, for the old man to bring his food.

The man who had offered Johnny fifty dollars to drop out of the bidding at the horse auction, the one Johnny thought of as the butler, entered the room, followed by a huge man who had to duck his head to enter. The two men came into the dark room and stopped, looking at Johnny sitting in the middle of the cell. The big man was the man Johnny had seen at the auction, standing close to Peterson and his group of henchmen.

"My name is Edwards. This is Mr. Jackson, he is the estate's foreman," said the smaller man, indicating the huge man, standing silently beside and slightly behind him. "I think you know why you find yourself here," continued the small man in his English accent.

"No, can't say that I do," said Johnny, without emotion.

"Is that so?" he replied. "Well, the fact that you are here indicates you're stupid so I guess it makes a kind of sense."

Johnny sat and looked at the big man, studying him. Over three hundred pounds, well over six feet tall and well into his forties, was Johnny's assessment.

"You were warned a number of times, not to bid on the horses," continued Edwards, his words clipped and precise.

"That's true," replied Johnny, as if agreeing the morning was cold.

"His Lordship was very upset."

When Johnny didn't respond, the man continued. "He has decided to give you a chance to appear before him and beg his forgiveness. If it will do any good, I cannot tell you. Like all great men, sometimes he is merciful, sometimes he feels the need to set an example. My advice to you is to be contrite. When you are afforded the opportunity, remove your hat and bow your head as you enter. When you are about ten feet from the master, stop and drop to your knees. Do not speak until you are spoken to."

Again, Johnny didn't respond, but his face showed astonishment. He thought the man must be joking around, but then, his situation wasn't a joke.

"However, the Marquis is a very busy man and has just returned from a trip. He will not be able to grant you an audience right away."

"I see," said Johnny. "Well, when do you reckon I'll be able to have a word with the great man?"

Edwards studied Johnny's face, to see if he was being sarcastic. He couldn't decide. "I don't know, but I think perhaps the first part of February."

"Well, then, while I'm waiting, could I possibly have some additional chow and maybe some cigarillos and matches?" Johnny asked, smiling. "Oh, and I could really use some coffee."

Rosalinda, her face somber, sat at the table and looked around her. Present were Henry Bear, his wife Venus, Jameson and Clyde. Her mother was tending to Lucrecia and her father had not returned from his own ranch, but was expected back soon.

Everyone had coffee in front of them and Clyde spoke, "If I may," he said, looking at Rosalinda.

"Please," she said.

"I sent telegrams to agents in New Orleans requesting them to check with city and parish law enforcement, to visit all hospitals and morgues.

Additionally, I requested they check all newspapers for personal ads." Noticing some questioning looks, he explained, "If a person has a loss of memory or perhaps we are dealing with a kidnapping for ransom situation, a news advertisement is sometimes used as a means of establishing contact."

Everyone nodded their understanding.

"I have spoken with the manager of the Menger hotel who knows Johnny personally and any messages sent to the Menger by Johnny or whom ever, will be forwarded to me personally at the St. James hotel in New Orleans."

Again, noticing questioning looks, Clyde said, "Mr. Jameson has told me the St. James is the hotel he and Johnny utilized during their stay, so I suggest we stay there and use it as our base of operations."

He paused, but when no one spoke, he continued. "Based on the information provided by Mr. Jameson, there is a possibility that a man named Peterson may be behind Johnny's disappearance. It seems unlikely the man would react in such a radical manner over the purchase of horses, but men often act in unpredictable ways. Whatever has happened, I am hopeful because it appears he has been kidnapped. It would have been easy enough for someone to shoot him or stab him in the street."

Clyde sipped his coffee. No one spoke. Rosalinda got up, took the coffee pot from the stove top and began re-filling the cups.

There was a knock at the door and Lupe, Rosalinda's father appeared. "Buenos dias todos."

Rosalinda smiled a weak smile and took a cup down from the shelf, filled it with coffee and handed it to him.

"I stopped by the Menger, there was no word," he said. There was silence and he said, "I better check on the mares," and he was gone.

Clyde said, "As to this Peterson fellow, I also asked an agent to find out all he could about the man." Nodding at Jameson, he continued, "Jameson tells me they were told the man inherited a two thousand-acre sugar plantation, is rich and a power in Louisiana state politics. Again, not a profile I would associate with someone who would harm a man in this instance. However, given the way Johnny was taken, by men wearing police uniforms, it is my thinking that just such a man would have the assets to pull off Johnny's kidnapping and disappearance. I have asked all the agents to telegraph me in Galveston. By the time we reach there, we should know more."

CHAPTER 30

Clyde, Jameson, Henry and Rosalinda sat, somber faced, as the stage coach bounced and rolled along toward Waelder on a cold, windy January morning. The train at Waelder was on time and everyone would have enjoyed the ride, especially Rosalinda and Henry who had never been on a train, if they didn't have constant thoughts of Johnny pressing on their minds.

There was a delay of five hours at Waelder and the group took refuge in a small café. The waitress, upon seeing Henry, disappeared into the back and the owner appeared and said Henry would have to leave, so they all left and waited at the train station. As they sat, without warning, Rosalinda said, "If Johnny had been with us they would have served Henry. He just has a way about him. Some kind of authority or something."

Jameson said, "Yes ma'am, he sure does."

They arrived in Galveston, but the ship they had booked passage on did not leave until the following day. After much discussion, against Rosalinda's protests, Henry said he would find a place to stay and helped the others carry their bags into the Tremont House, a beautiful hotel that Clyde had stayed in the year before. Rosalinda asked for the manager and after a private word, she stepped over to Henry and said, "The manager has agreed to let you use an empty room in the hotel worker's hallway."

"Thank you, ma'am. I am much obliged."

To Jameson's great surprise not only did he not suffer any seasickness on the trip to New Orleans, but neither did any of the other three. Again, everyone found the voyage and the ship interesting, but their fear and concern over Johnny kept them in a state of anxiety.

Arriving at the St. James hotel in New Orleans, Rosalinda inquired and found a hotel not far away that served blacks and mulattos. There were a number of messages for Clyde and he told the group they should meet in an hour, after he had time to read and digest them. Again, Rosalinda inquired and was given a name of a restaurant that allowed blacks and mulattos.

"Ma'am," said the hotel manager, "there will not be many, if any whites."

"Fine, thank you," said Rosalinda, decked out in a dress and hat. "I'm not white myself, if you notice."

Jameson, Rosalinda and Clyde met in the hotel lobby. It was easy to tell from Clyde's face that there had been no word from Johnny. After they had met up with Henry and ordered supper, Clyde said, "In a way, there is good news. No one matching Johnny's description has been discovered in the morgue. The police and sheriff have no record of him ever being arrested. No notices in the newspapers."

"What about this Peterson fellow?" asked Jameson.

"Ah," said Clyde, "an interesting individual by all accounts. He calls himself Lord Peterson, hinting that he is a Marquis of something or other in France. Some kind of inherited title. His great-grandfather established a sugar plantation, which was inherited by his father and now belongs to him. As Jameson was told, he seems to be very wealthy and my agent says he is well known and a powerful force behind the scenes within the Democratic Party here in Louisiana."

Clyde paused and looked around. The waiter appeared and served them. After he left, Clyde continued, "What is interesting are the rumors. Folks say he still operates his sugar plantation with slave labor," holding up his hand, he continued, "I know, it's also rumored he is protected by the authorities and if someone crosses him, they have been known to disappear."

It was Henry that said what they were all thinking. "That don't sound good Mr. Clyde."

"The fact is, and I am sorry to be so blunt, but if Mr. Black is dead, there is nothing we can do about that, except bring those responsible to justice. If he is alive, he needs help and we must find him."

"So what do we do now?" asked Jameson.

"We must go to Peterson's sugar plantation and look for Johnny. It is doubtful we would be welcomed, so we shall have to devise a way to do it without being detected. One of the details in the report says that there may be seventy or more blacks working and living on Peterson's property. Henry, I'm thinking if you can find a way to get on the property and talk to some of the workers, maybe they can tell you if there's a place where a prisoner might be held."

"Yes! I can do that," said Henry.

"Mr. Bear," said Clyde, "understand, you can't just ride in and announce yourself nor can you let any of the men in charge see you."

Smiling, Henry replied, "I was a slave, most of my life. I know how to do it. I'll go at night, visit the folks in their quarters."

The door banged open and Johnny woke up. He sat up as a white man came in, opened the cell door on the cage next to his where George had been held. The man stood back as two black men came in holding another black man between them. They took him into the cell and laid him down and then stepped out. The white man, one Johnny had not seen before, locked the door to the cage and left. Johnny heard the bolt on the outside door slam shut.

Johnny waited, but the man didn't move, so he went back to sleep. When he awoke five or six hours later, the man was sitting up and in the dim light, Johnny could see his face was swollen and bloody. "Good afternoon," said Johnny.

The man turned his eyes toward Johnny. "I thought maybe you was dead," said the man. "What's a white man doing in here anyways?"

"I seem to have made Lord Peterson angry," explained Johnny.

"I buried a white man not six months ago out in the new field. Don't know what he done, but folks, my folks, the black people, say he was killed in the big house. He was very bloody. Cuts on his face and arms and his shirt and body all cut to shreds. Never seen nothing like it."

"Are you going to be all right?" asked Johnny.

"I reckon so. Mr. Jackson say he don't like the way I look at him. He beat me pretty good. This is the first time I been in the stockade, but other folk say you don't get no food for three days. I expect I can last three days. My name is Daniel by the way."

"Pleased to make your acquaintance Daniel, I'm Johnny."

The next morning, the old man slid Johnny's tin plate under the cell bars and as he did, he dropped a small sack and a sweet potato on the ground. When the old man had left and Johnny heard the door being locked, he went over to the bars between him and Daniel and holding the potato, he stuck his hand through the bars. Smiling, Daniel took it and thanked Johnny.

"I have some cornbread and salt pork; we can split that."

"No thank you sir. I appreciate it, but I'll be fine. Thank you for the potato." He smiled. "I'll eat half of it today and half tomorrow. I'll be fine."

Johnny found a small sack of tobacco, some rolling papers and four matches in the small bag. Once again he went to the bars and offered half to Daniel, who refused, noting he'd be released in a couple of days, but no telling how long Johnny was going to be there.

"They won't hold me long, there's too much work to be done. I didn't look at Mr. Jackson funny, he just putting fear into everybody least they get ideas."

"There was a fellow in here, name of George," said Johnny, "do you know if he's okay?"

"Yes sir, he fine. He be wearing leg irons now, cause he try to run away."

"Yes, he said he took a horse," replied Johnny. "I'd a thought he might have got away."

Laughing now, Daniel said, "Mr. Johnny, we on a big place, surrounded by countryside and they got the dogs after him."

"Dogs?" responded Johnny.

"Oh yes sir. Lord Peterson himself lead the hunt. He enjoy it."

CHAPTER 31

"I don't think it wise to go about asking about Johnny," said Clyde. "At least until we know if Peterson is involved. It's best if word doesn't get to him that we are here, looking for Johnny."

"Are we to just sit here?" exclaimed Rosalinda.

Clyde looked at her. "I realize your despair, but we must develop a plan. I think it's best if you see a bit of the city. If you stay on the main streets during the day, I feel that you'll be safe."

"What will you three be doing?"

"After I obtain a map, we'll procure some horses and ride as close as possible to Peterson's plantation, so we can get a feel for it. We'll try to find an entry point for Henry."

"I will accompany you," said Rosalinda, her voice firm.

Sighing, Clyde replied, "As you wish, but I need a few hours. Why don't you three see something of the city, perhaps the French Quarter? Henry won't stand out there. Let's meet here at noon tomorrow for dinner."

Johnny felt sure he could trust Daniel, but he didn't dig until three days later, after Daniel was removed from his cell and taken away. Johnny continued to be given a plate of food, always cornbread and salt pork, once a day, but the morning Daniel was released, the old man dropped a sweet potato in his cell again. Johnny was beyond thankful. That night, he began digging again.

Sometime in the wee hours of the morning, Johnny took a break, rolling a cigarette, his first since the old man had left him the tobacco, papers and matches. He had been waiting, savoring the thought of smoking. As he sat and enjoyed the smoke, his mind went to what Daniel had said about George being tracked down by dogs. This was something Johnny hadn't considered and it made his situation much more dire. He knew, well, he felt that if he could escape he'd have a reasonable chance of getting away. One problem however, was that he felt himself getting weaker each day from lack of food. It would affect his stamina if he had to walk a long distance, especially if he had to try to move quickly, before the dogs found his trail.

Returning to his digging, he realized he was making progress. In another few nights he should be able to start digging under the logs. Hopefully, in a week or so, he would break through on the other side, timing it for just after nightfall. He could crawl out and have the entire night to travel before it was discovered he'd escaped.

The next morning, Rosalinda, Jameson and Henry walked the streets of New Orleans, marveling at the strangeness of the city. They walked past blacks speaking French and admired the French and Spanish Creole influenced buildings.

When the three returned to the restaurant, they found Clyde sitting at the same table.

Looking up, Clyde said, "Shall we order?"

As the group ate, Clyde said, "Rosalinda, I am expending a great deal of funds which may well all be for naught."

"As I told you, spare no expense," said Rosalinda and Clyde nodded.

"After we've finished our meal, let's adjourn to my room for privacy."

An hour later, the group was gathered in Clyde's room. Rosalinda sat in the only chair, Henry and Jameson, at Clyde's request, sat on the bed and Clyde stood holding a map.

"The map is rather vague, but I have an idea of where we are going. According to the records in the General Land Office, Peterson's plantation is roughly two miles by two miles, some two thousand and five hundred acres. The surrounding area is agricultural; predominantly sugar, cotton, corn and livestock. It is not heavily populated and there are few roads. I think it's best if we develop a story in the event we find ourselves in conversation with someone or if we're observed on the road. Gossip can be dangerous, especially for us. To be frank, we're a strange appearing group. Rosalinda, a beautiful Mexican woman, Henry, a rather large, middle-aged black man, myself, an older white man and Mr. Jameson, himself an older white man."

Jameson chuckled. "You just as well say it all out loud. Me and you are older white men, but you look like a banker and I'm a down-in-the-heel cowboy. We sure as hell don't match up well."

Clyde smiled. "Appearances can be deceiving," he said, "and that is what we must put to our advantage. I must warn everyone. With what little information we have, we can only make a plan and trust it goes well, because we cannot foresee what will occur." He paused and looked around the room. "I think, regarding all I have heard about Peterson and his men; we must all be armed. Rosalinda, are you?"

She interrupted him. "I am quite comfortable with firearms and brought my personal handgun."

Nodding, Clyde continued, "I have a rough plan, working on the assumption that Johnny is being held prisoner by Peterson. That said, we need to get Henry onto the plantation without anyone seeing him. Once there, he can try to discover if Peterson is holding Johnny prisoner. If he is, then Henry will try to locate and if possible free Johnny and bring him back to a pre-planned pickup point. If he is unable to free him, we will recover Henry and make a new plan based on the intelligence he provides.

When no one spoke, Clyde folded the map and placed it on the wash basin, then stooped and opened the lid on a small wooden box sitting on the floor. He reached in, and standing straight, lifted his hand, which now held a Bible. "You said I look like a banker. Would I pass as a Bible salesman?"

Everyone sat, a bit stunned, then Henry's face broke out in a huge smile. "I think you look more like a Bible salesman than an investigator," he said.

"This afternoon, I made arrangements to rent a horse. In the morning, I'll ride the area around the plantation and hopefully identify an entry point for Henry. So as not to raise any suspicions, I will visit some homes and try to sell some Bibles, asking directions at each place to the nearby homes. At some point I will approach the Peterson house and see what I can see. I doubt they'll welcome me, but I am going to attempt to be invited in. I want to get a feel for the house in the event Johnny is being held there. If it comes to it and we have to recover him by force, perhaps I can get a sense of how many men Peterson has hanging about."

"Mr. Jameson, use this afternoon and tomorrow, if you will, to locate and purchase an enclosed wagon and one horse to pull it. You'll also need a few goods and some pans, shovels and the like to hang from the sides of it."

Jameson looked at Clyde, his face a mask of confusion.

Smiling, Clyde said, "We all need a plausible reason to be in the area and we need a place to hide Johnny, should we find him. You will be a drummer who was accosted by highwaymen, say in the western part of the state. They stole your wagon, horse and all your goods. You must now replace them. Once you have outfitted properly and our plan has taken shape, we will hide Henry in the wagon and you will drop him off at the edge of the Peterson estate so he can try to make contact."

Clyde had everyone's attention, but no one spoke. "Rosalinda, one of the local agents is, as we speak, in the process of obtaining a nun's habit." Rosalinda's face showed surprise. "For our purposes you will become a Catholic nun. I will be a priest. I have arranged to rent a small buggy and horse from another local man. This will give us a reason to be on the road and in the area. If Henry finds Johnny and they are able to escape or if he returns alone, they will get in Jameson's wagon. You and I will be posted on the same road and can be pretending to visit with Jameson. If Henry returns with Johnny, we will leave first and drive along a quarter mile in front.

There will be searches on the roads if Johnny is a prisoner and is discovered missing. If we come upon searchers, we will stop and speak to the men as a diversion. We will tell them we are visiting the sick. Hopefully, coming behind us, Jameson will have time to stop and let Henry and Johnny hide on the side of the road. If he is stopped by searchers and they want to search the wagon, well, it may come down to gunplay. I know the plan is full of maybes and holes, but we will have to adapt as need be. I only hope we find Johnny."

Everyone sat and digested his words for a minute, then continuing he said, "Henry, I'm thinking if Peterson has as many black folks on his plantation as I've heard, it's possible that if you're discovered, you'll be mistaken for one of them. You'll need to wear, well, poor clothing I think."

"Yes sir, you're right. No slave or for that matter any black man, would be dressed as well as I am. Leave it to me, I'll lay my hands on what I need."

"The local agents I have engaged are monitoring their contacts with the police and doctors. They will contact me here at the hotel in the event they have news. Tomorrow I will assume my role as a Bible salesman and if the rest of you will complete your assignments, we will meet again tomorrow evening in my room, say eight o'clock?"

Friday morning, when the old man brought in Johnny's food, he squatted down, pushed the tin under the bars, pulled something from his pocket and slid it under the plate. Johnny didn't move until the old man had left and he heard the door bolt slam. Picking up his plate, he saw a small, flat, rusted piece of metal. Picking it up and examining it, he realized it was a piece of an old hoe. It would be a great help in the digging. Smiling, he bit into the hunk of cornbread and his teeth closed on something. Looking at the cornbread, he realized a small, folded piece of paper had been hidden in it. Unfolding it, he saw crude writing on it. '*Bos say Lord see you on da Sabbath*'.

Johnny was stunned. It was, he thought, a Friday. He only had two days to make good his escape. Johnny sat, motionless. The old man, bless him, must have realized why Johnny wanted the spoon. 'Lord' could only be Peterson or else he was going to be killed and meet his maker. Either way, he had to work faster.

Chapter 32

The cook found a tall stool for Caleb to sit on, so he could keep his bad leg straight. He was out of laudanum and thought come the weekend, he'd see if he could get B.R. to take him back to the doctor in the wagon, maybe get some more. B.R. had used his straight razor and fingers to cut and pull out his stitches. His hair was growing back over the slash on the side of his head where the doctor had shaved it and sewed up his wound, but his face held traces of the bruising. Middle of the week, the foreman came in, had a word with the cook and B.R. was told to report out to the barn to help with the care of the horses held there. Brushing, feeding and doctoring for those being held close. A dozen mares, a piebald gelding that had been bitten by something, leaving a nasty wound and a few horses with various needs. There was the occasional shoeing or branding, and the tack needed rubbing down. There was always work to be done.

As he passed Caleb, who was cutting up vegetables and cubing some beef steak for a stew, he slapped him on the shoulder. That night, as the two sat on a big rock by the creek, smoking, B.R. said, "I don't know why you're so dang glum. Another month they'll move you to my place in the barn and I'll be back branding longhorns and breaking horses."

"It ain't that, and you know it," replied Caleb. "I thought we had a connection, me and Mollie. She makes me laugh and I enjoy being with her. I feel like a fool. Buying her drinks and telling her stuff about me."

When B.R. didn't reply, Caleb continued, "Anyhow, you're a fine one to talk. That girl never gave you the time of day and you're carrying on like, well, like a lovesick rooster."

"How exactly does a lovesick rooster act?" asked B.R.

"I don't rightly know. It just came to me."

B.R. laughed. "I don't reckon you can make somebody care about you," he said, "but you know what Caleb, I'm a mite stubborn, so I reckon I'll try one more time. Maybe tell her I like her. See what happens. It'll be the last time."

"You know what's odd, Billy Ray, we known a lot of pretty girls, you and me. How come we never fell for any of them?"

"If I knew that secret; the secret of attraction; the love spell. I'd sell it and be a rich gentleman 'stead of a broke bronc-buster."

"You believe in fate Billy Ray? What's going to happen is going to happen."

"Nope, I surely don't, but I do believe we have choices and that folks give us messages and touch our lives. It's up to us to decide."

"Angels, that what you're saying?"

"I don't know Caleb. Could be sometimes angels bring us messages. You know, folks always giving us advice and such. We just ignore most of it."

"That's pretty deep. How about luck?"

"I've heard a man makes his own luck," but turning to look at Caleb and smiling, he continued, "but yeah, I believe in luck."

Saturday afternoon, B.R. borrowed the ranch wagon, telling the foreman he was taking Caleb to the doctor to get his hip checked. That was true, but Caleb was really hoping for some laudanum. He could buy some if he could find an apothecary somewhere, at least he thought he could. He'd never wanted any before.

Arriving in San Antonio, the two men took a room for the night and then headed for the doctor's office. The doctor examined Caleb and asked about pain and use of his leg. Finished, he stepped back and seemed satisfied. "Caleb, I think you are going to heal up okay. I'd give it another two or three weeks before I really put it to the test. Now, I don't mean busting horses. That's months in the future."

Caleb nodded and said, "Doc, I was thinking I could use some more medicine, to help me sleep and work."

The doctor studied him. Finally, he said, "Caleb, I can sell you another bottle, but I must caution you. Some folks get to depending on it and well, it's like becoming a drunk. There's no going back."

Caleb looked at the doctor and out of the corner of his eye, he could see B.R. staring at him. After a moment, said, "Thank ye kindly, I reckon I'll get by without it."

"Well," said B.R., "I'm thinking to take my last shot. You coming along?"

"B.R., if you don't mind, drop me off close to the Grand. There's a place close by advertises the biggest beef steak in town. I thinking to eat there and have a drink at the Grand."

B.R. was about to shake the reins and get the horse moving, but he was so surprised, he didn't move. "Do you mean it? Whatever for?"

"I just want to see her one last time."

"There's just no explaining us dumb-ass cowboys," said B.R. clucking the horses into action.

At the restaurant, B.R. helped Caleb off the wagon and Caleb said, "If things go your way, I'll see you in the room, if not come on by and we'll drink our sorrows away."

B.R. took the wagon to a wagon yard and paid to leave it and have the horses seen to, then he caught a ride with a freighter, driving a wagon pulled by two oxen, who dropped him off close to the Café del Rio. Entering, he was surprised to see Topsannah's father-in-law waiting on the tables.

"Excuse me sir," said B.R. "Is Topsannah about?"

Looking harried, he replied, "No, she is at home, sick."

"Sick," said B.R., alarmed.

"Si," patting his hand to his head, he continued, "fierbre."

"Oh," responded B.R. "Fever. I sure hope it's not serious."

"Doctor Hernandez say fiebre de invierno, she sick, ten, eleven days now. Doctor say she is better, will be well soon. I must go, dishes piling up, very busy. Cousin not able to help today."

"Winter fever! I'm sorry I didn't come last week," exclaimed B.R., who stood for a moment processing the information. He had heard that winter fever killed folks, but she was better. Then coming out of his thoughts, he said, "Why I'm right experienced at doing dishes," as he suddenly headed through the door to the kitchen where he found the mother-in-law cooking frantically. Stacks of dirty cups, plates, pots and pans sat on a counter by a deep sink. By the time he had water boiling on one of the stove's burners, he had the dishes scrapped and organized. He had discovered both baking soda and several bottles of something he had never seen before: *Sheppard's Improved Liquid Soap.* Rolling up his sleeves, he went to work scrubbing the dishes in the hot water and dropping them in a pan of clean water.

The stacks of dishes rose and fell through the late afternoon and early evening. B.R. did not stop to eat or smoke. Finally, he stepped out into the dining room and taking the coffee pot from Topsannah's father-in-law, told him to rest a few minutes. The man smiled, and said, "Gracias."

Most of their customers were Mexican and those that spoke to him did so in Spanish. He missed a few words, but he was fluent enough to get by. He began to take orders, picked up plates and delivered the hot dishes of food and in between, refilled coffee cups. Entering the kitchen to grab the next order, he saw the father-in-law cooking and the mother-in-law sitting, resting. She smiled at him.

"We've got enough dishes for the night," he told the father-in-law. "You stay and help back here; I'll handle the customers."

Finally, the last customer out the door and the door bolted, B.R. exhausted, tackled the dishes and after two hours, had them all clean, dry and stacked. Topsannah's mother-in-law and father-in-law had cleaned the restaurant and organized the food. B.R. retrieved his hat and nodded to them.

The man tried to pay him and B.R. refused. "I'm glad to help. Please tell Topsannah, I hope she feels better."

Once outside, B.R. built himself a cigarette and started for the Grand Saloon. He figured Caleb had long since gone to the room, but he wanted a drink or two.

Using a cane now, Caleb worked his way into the saloon and found his usual table at the back, empty. Noticing him, the bartender brought him a glass of beer, but Caleb barely noticed him as he scanned the room for Mollie. There, he saw her, talking to a man at the bar. Noticing him, she said something to the man she was talking to, smiled and began walking toward Caleb's table.

Reaching the table, she stood for a moment and then said, "Hello Cal."

"My name is Caleb," he said quietly.

She didn't look surprised, but continued to stand and look at him. "Cal, ah, Caleb, I, well, I'm sorry for ignoring you the last time you were here, but I was entertaining a man and couldn't get free."

"It ain't none of my affair," said Caleb. "I'm a customer like everybody else what buys you drinks so you'll smile at 'em."

"Would you like me to sit?" she asked.

"Might as well," said Caleb, "I don't see your man about," his voice cold. As he looked toward the bar, he saw the bartender looking his way, and he motioned.

"He is not my man, Caleb," replied Mollie, a hint of anger in her voice. "And why did you tell me your name was Cal? Are you married?"

Surprised at having the situation turned on him, Caleb said "No I ain't married."

Mollie looked at him.

"All right, if you must know," he said, lifting his hat up to reveal his blond hair, "I'm the fellow was charged with murdering Lila."

Mollie's eyes went wide and her mouth formed a circle.

Setting his hat back down on his head, he continued, "I hope you've heard it weren't me that killed her. I've been cleared."

Mollie, still in shock, nodded her affirmation. "I didn't realize," she uttered.

"I come around to try to find information to clear my name," he said. "That's how come I started talking to you and used a different name. But an investigator found out who really done it and along the way, well, along the way I come to enjoy your company."

Mollie's face was a mix of emotions. She ignored the drink the bartender had sat in front of her. Caleb, looking away, sipped his warm beer. Finally, he pulled out his makings and began to build a smoke.

"Caleb, I've enjoyed your company."

He lit his quirly, shook the match out and looked at her, disbelief on his face.

"Any no how, I just wanted to come by and tell you goodbye. I'm thinking I'll be moving on."

Her face falling, Mollie replied, "Where will you go? Is your family really deceased?"

"Yes, everything I told you is true, well, you know, except for my name. I reckon I may go to California. Never been there."

Mollie studied him. "Caleb, I want to tell you something, but if you repeat it, well, you could put my life in danger."

This caught Caleb completely unawares. "What are you talking about? Is someone after you?"

"No, but they would be, if they knew what I'm about."

Caleb began to shake his head. "Don't tell me. I don't do well in jail, and I'm not interested in anything might put me back in there."

She looked at him, puzzled and then smiled. "No silly, I'm not talking about a crime. Well, I am, but, well, let me explain."

Suddenly, she picked up her watered-down drink and swallowed it in one gulp. "Order us another before I begin," she said, her voice stressed.

Caleb got up, walked to the bar and returned with two whiskeys. Sitting down, he said, "I paid the bartender for four 'drinks' for you, so I reckon we're good for a bit. Are you fixing to tell me a tall tale?"

She looked at him, her face somber. "No Caleb. I'm going to tell you about the death of my father."

"My name is really Mollie," she began, "but I'm not here to make money. I came here to kill the man you saw me with."

It was Caleb's turn to be shocked. "What?" he uttered.

"I'm from Missouri; my father owned a bank. One day, I was in his office visiting when one of the clerks called to my father and he stepped out of the office to see what was needed. I heard yelling and a shot. I ran to the door and one of the men," she hesitated, "was holding a gun. His kerchief slipped down and I saw him clearly. They ran away with the cash from the teller's drawer. My father was dead."

Caleb reached across the table and squeezed her hand. "I'm sorry," he said, quietly.

"The sheriff and a posse chased them for a day, but didn't catch them. The sheriff showed me a wanted poster with the man's face on it. It seems they were known bank robbers, but had never been caught."

Caleb and Mollie sat and sipped their drinks, each lost in their own thoughts. Then Caleb looked at her and was about to speak when she said, "I know you're wondering how I ended up here, in San Antonio,

Texas. I read every paper and visited the sheriff until he took to hiding when he saw me coming. I just wanted to know if my father's killer had been caught or killed."

She sipped her drink, bit her lower lip, then continued. "There were bank robberies around the country, but not as many as you might think. I noticed that if you wanted to, you could see a pattern in some of the holdups. They seemed to be moving south and west, about as fast as one might travel by horse. I began to wonder if the man who killed my father and his gang were perhaps robbing banks as they headed for the territories. I started seeking out the papers in all the western and southern towns, and it wasn't easy, but there was a robbery in Dallas and I hired a Pinkerton man to look into it for me. He telegraphed me that there had been another, more recent bank robbery in Austin. So I headed this way with the crazy idea I might find him; the man who killed my father. But actually, working with the wanted poster I sent him, the Pinkerton man discovered him here, in San Antonio, by going from saloon to saloon and paying the bartenders to look at the poster. So, I got a job here to get close to him, so I could kill him, but I realized, when the time came I couldn't do it."

Caleb had sat, spellbound as he listened to the story.

"The man you saw me with is the man who killed my father."

"You were sitting in his lap. You kissed him," said Caleb, his voice incredulous.

"I have been befriending him, to get close so I can kill him. It worked. He asked me to come to his room, twice. The last time, was the night you saw me. It was my chance, but as I said, I realized I just couldn't do it. Then, just as I was about to leave his table, I heard them talking about the First State. There is a First State Bank here and maybe they're planning to rob it. decided to stay close and see if I can pick up more information. That's what I was doing when you saw me. Hoping he'd relax and say something else."

Caleb said, "That's the doggone strangest story I've ever heard. What kind of woman are you?"

"Smart, determined,?" she ventured.

"I was thinking scary," replied Caleb, his face serious.

"I am telling you the gospel truth. I went to the sheriff with the wanted poster, but he said Missouri was a long way away and there was nothing to link the man to any crime in Bexar county. I told him about the men discussing the First State Bank. He couldn't stop himself laughing at me. Told me I should join the Pinkertons if I wanted to play detective. But I know banks and I went to the First State and talked to the manager. He's hired a guard, to stay in the back, just in case."

Caleb sat, staring at her, his face twisted in thought.

"Caleb, I was married and my husband did die in the war. I wanted you to know," she paused, looking at him. "I'm glad you came, Caleb. This is my last night of work here. I've told the bartender my mother is ill and I have to return home, just in case someone inquires. I don't want the gang members to be suspicious. I'll stay in town for a while, just to see if they really do try to rob the bank and then I'll head home."

Caleb looked alarmed. "Home," he said. "I was thinking maybe we could, ah, have supper together or something."

"I thought you were going to California," said Mollie.

"Oh, yeah, ah, I am," he said, noticing his cane propped against his chair. "As soon as my hip heals up. I got throwed by a real bad horse and hurt it. I just saw the doctor and I can't ride for a while yet."

Mollie smiled.

Entering the Grand Saloon, B.R. figured Caleb would either gone to the room, or he'd still be here and be drunk, so he wasn't surprised to see him sitting alone at a table, clearly drunk.

What surprised B.R. was the stupid grin on Caleb's face. Must be the whiskey, he thought, as he headed for the table.

Flopping on the chair across from Caleb, B.R. said, "I can tell you're drowning your sorrows. Just don't start puking."

Caleb smiled at B.R. "You was a long-time getting here. Was you sparking Topsannah? You must have done; but what she could see in a dirt-poor, bronc-busting cowboy and ugly to boot, I just don't know."

"You are drunk," said B.R. "No, I wasn't courting Topsannah. I was working. She's laid up with the winter fever and I was helping out at the café."

This got through the fog of alcohol and Caleb sat up straight. "The winter fever!" he exclaimed.

"Easy amigo, it's okay. The worst of it has passed. Her father-in-law said she's had it for nigh on two weeks and she's better."

"You gave me a scare. Folks die from winter fever." Frowning, Caleb said, "How was it you was helping at the café? You can't cook, hell, you burned the beans last time you tried to cook."

"I washed dishes, mainly," said B.R. "But never mind about me. You're awfully happy for a man who come to say goodbye to a girl he favors."

Caleb smiled. "Mollie and I are planning to step out next Saturday night."

"You ain't right, I can see that," said B.R. "Where is the lady?"

"She's somewhere about, you know, talking to men. It's all an act."

"What? You're not making much sense, but I'm bone tired. What say we call it a night?"

Caleb didn't have a chance to answer before there was a shout at the faro table where men stood three deep. As Caleb and B.R. turned to look in the direction of the outburst, all hell broke loose. Caleb swayed slightly as he stood up and a chair came flying through the air, missing him by inches and crashing against the wall. Caleb abruptly sat down again. For a full minute, men wrestled and punched each other, cursing and yelling.

Someone crashed against the table where Caleb and B.R. sat, their glasses toppling to the floor. Someone yelled, "Knife!" B.R. jumped to his feet, grabbed Caleb by the arm and shouted, "Let's go!"

B.R. picked Caleb's cane up and handed it to him. They had just cleared the door as two men pushed past them and they heard a gunshot from inside the saloon. Caleb suddenly jerked his arm away from B.R. and called out, "Mollie!" as he headed back inside the saloon.

B.R. grabbed him around the shoulders and said, "Come on, she'll be fine."

Caleb continued to struggle, but suddenly, three more shots rang out and he and B.R. froze.

Caleb lurched back inside the saloon, dropped his cane and fell twice, but B.R. helped him to his feet. Men were pouring out the door, in a hurry to get away. Two uniformed city marshals, part of the new force organized in San Antonio by the new city marshal the year before, appeared and fought their way into the saloon as Caleb and B.R. looked about for Mollie.

A small group of men was huddled around someone on the floor. Looking around they saw several women in the corner.

"Caleb!" shouted Mollie, appearing beside them, her lip bloody, grabbing Caleb in a hug.

"You're hurt," said Caleb, trying to push her back, so he could look at her face.

"Just my lip," she replied, smiling at him. "I got hit in the melee."

B.R. sighed. Mollie's face had lit up when she saw Caleb, and judging from his friend's reaction, it looked to him like the two were in love.

The next morning, a Sunday, Caleb and B.R rolled out late after their night at the Grand Saloon, but when they packed up and left the room, they headed for the Café del Rio. B.R. still wasn't clear how things had worked out with Mollie. Caleb tried to explain it on the way to the room the night before, but made little sense. He had said she wasn't a saloon girl, but that didn't figure. She was working as a saloon girl.

Caleb was in some distress as a result of his night of drinking and he walked in silence. B.R. was also quiet, but he was thinking that he hadn't had a chance to tell Topsannah how he felt and wondering if he should wait until she was well over her illness or try to do it as soon as she returned to work.

The two men stepped into the café and were greeted by a Mexican woman they didn't know. "Buenos dias," they said in unison.

As they sat, B.R. looked about for Topsannah and felt his disappointment when he didn't see her, although he knew she would still be home in bed. The father-in-law brought their plates of food and smiling at B.R. said, "Topsannah much better this morning. She want to work, but I say no. I tell her you help all night. She very surprised, say if I see you, tell you 'muchas gracias'.

B.R.'s face beamed. After the two men ate, they walked to the wagon yard and were soon on their way to the Circle C, each lost in his own thoughts of what lay ahead.

Caleb was in equal parts excited and happy for himself, looking forward to seeing Mollie soon, but he was also concerned that B.R. was courting heartbreak. The man was trying to win a woman who was part Comanche, part Mexican and didn't seem to care one bit for him.

When the headache he was suffering eased, Caleb told B.R. Mollie's story.

"You reckon it's the gospel truth?" asked B.R.

"I believe her," said Caleb. "If you sit with her, she acts like, well, like a saloon girl, but when she relaxes, you can tell she's had an education. She knows a lot about books and history and the like."

B.R., holding the reins, the horses walking, the day cold, but clear, digested this new information. "Well, I'll be," he finally said. Then, after a minute of thought, continued, "Caleb, if she's educated and the daughter of a banker, how you reckon she's gonna take to the life of a broke cowboy?"

"I hadn't thought much about that," replied Caleb, "but I guess I better."

CHAPTER 33

On Friday, as Johnny slept, Clyde, having visited four homesteads and selling one Bible, was on the Peterson estate, riding up a lane with large trees on both sides. One of the neighbors had cautioned him, telling him it would be best if he avoided the place.

"They aren't neighborly. In fact they threatened me a few months ago. I was just trying to find a hog of mine that got loose and you'd a thought I was destroying the place the way they carried on. No sir, I'd go an extra ten miles for help afore I'd set foot on their place again."

"Thank you," said Clyde. "I appreciate the warning, but I'm the Lord's shepherd and it's my duty to spread the word. You folks have a joyous day."

He rode slowly, taking in everything he could see. Through the trees, perhaps a half-mile away, Clyde could see wooden cabins, built in two rows. These would have been the slave quarters or perhaps, if the rumors were true, thought Clyde, still were. He saw two black men cross the road ahead of him. One was carrying cane poles, the other had a string of fish slung over his shoulder. Catfish and a large gar, as best as he could tell. Veering off the lane, he walked his horse into the woods, toward the cabins, and when he was well into the trees, dismounted. Leaning against a tree, he relieved himself. In the event someone challenged him, he wanted a reason for being off the road. Standing there, he studied the cabins. There were two rows and every cabin appeared to have two chimneys and two doors in the front. Built to hold two families, thought Clyde as he studied the area around the cabins. He saw two women tending a large garden and there, a shed, no it was a chicken coop, he realized.

He had seen the sugarcane fields earlier as he skirted the plantation. As he feared, as he moved around the plantation and stopped to observe with his spyglass, he had seen at least six men on horseback, carrying rifles, just walking their horses or sitting them. Guards, no doubt. The harvest was done and the fields full of stubs. Clyde had heard that in the West Indies, the fields were burned after the harvest, but he hadn't heard of it being done in America. He tied the horse's reins to a tree branch and moved through the trees. Seeing the roof of another building, he moved until he could see it better. He had left the spyglass in his bags, as he didn't want to be caught using it. The building was a large structure and blacks, men and women, were moving in and out of it and around it. He saw a white man gesturing at something. The sugarhouse, where they process the cane, thought Clyde.

He walked back to his horse, mounted and reentering the lane, continued. Rounding a curve, he could see a large house, with tall white columns. Ah, the great-house at last, he thought. He didn't see any stables, but this was a large estate. They were likely somewhere to the rear of the house. As he neared the house, he could see it was larger than his first impression. It was, considered Clyde, a story and a half. Likely the bedrooms were all upstairs.

Clyde tied his horse to a tree and approached the house, stepping up on the large porch, listening and observing, a brand-new Bible in his greatcoat pocket. He was dressed in his normal gray suit, which he thought befitted a Bible salesman.

He used the large ornate knocker to announce his presence and in less than a minute, the large door opened and a man, dressed in a black suit, with a starched white shirt, peered at Clyde as though he were cow dung. In an English accent, the man asked, "Why are you here?"

"Good day sir!" exclaimed Clyde. "How are you? I am here as a messenger of the Lord."

The man frowned as though Clyde were speaking a foreign language. "You have a message from the Lord?" asked the man.

Clyde immediately understood that the man thought he was referring to 'Lord Peterson'.

"Oh yes," said Clyde. "Perhaps I might have a glass of water or a cup of coffee. I've been traveling all day."

The man, Clyde had decided he must be the butler, looked annoyed, but looked around and seeing no one to help him, said, "Yes, step in if you please and let me show you to the drawing room."

Clyde, hat in hand, stepped into a hallway, with an expensive rug, expensive paper on the walls and a beautiful grandfather clock. He followed the man down the hall and into a large room with a couch and chairs, although no fire was lit in the large fireplace.

"Is the message urgent?" asked the butler, hesitating to leave Clyde.

"Oh yes, he's coming earlier than you expect," said Clyde, earnestly.

Frowning, the butler replied, "We're expecting him Sunday morning. If he is arriving home earlier, not later, why did he send you?"

Clyde was thoroughly enjoying himself now. "There is much to be done before he returns," responded Clyde, smiling.

"I see," said the butler. "I'll just be a moment," and he left the room. Clyde rose and walked to the window and parting the heavy drapes with one hand, he looked out onto the back of the house. There, a hundred yards away, stood a two-story structure. The servant's quarters, thought Clyde and he could see a bunkhouse, two white men standing outside smoking and talking. Facing the door to the bunkhouse, but fifty yards away, sat the stables and he could see an outhouse.

A black woman, who must have exited from the back door of the house appeared, walking out toward the servant's quarters in the rear. She stopped when a huge white man appearing on the trail as he passed some trees, appeared to yell at her and she lowered her head.

Turning away from the window, Clyde studied the room. Several huge paintings of men in French military uniforms adorned the walls. The butler appeared with a cup of coffee in a china cup with a china saucer. He set in on a small table close to the chair where Clyde had been sitting.

"Sir, may I have the message now?" asked the butler.

"Certainly," said Clyde. "The Lord was clear. He'll be returning sooner than we expect and we must repent and mend our ways if we're to be saved. With that in mind, I am offering folks a brand-new Bible for the low cost of five dollars." Clyde pulled the Bible from his coat pocket and held it up. "A small sum to pay for help in entering Heaven," he continued.

The butler was stunned and didn't speak for several seconds. "You are a salesman?" he asked.

"I am a messenger spreading the word," said Clyde, sipping his coffee.

Right before Clyde's eyes, the butler appeared to turn purple, then he screamed a name. Clyde sipped his coffee. Two younger men appeared, dressed somewhat like the butler and the butler shouted at them, "Throw this man out of the house!"

Staring at Clyde, well-dressed and sipping coffee, they were confused, but when the butler screamed "Now!" the two men approached Clyde, grabbed him by the arms and hustled him to the front door and heaved him off the porch, sending him sprawling. A second later, the butler, appearing on the porch holding the Bible Clyde had left in the drawing room, threw it at him. Calmly, Clyde arose, picked up the Bible, put it in his pocket and dusted himself off.

As he looked back at the house, the butler and the two men were standing frozen in place, glaring at him.

"Thank you for the coffee," said Clyde, turning and walking to his horse. As he rode away, he noticed the three men had been joined by the very large man he had seen approaching the house from the back.

CHAPTER 34

Friday evening, Clyde stood, studying the group. They were once again assembled in his room. Rosalinda looked tired, her face showing signs of strain. Henry Bear look grim and Jameson, well, he looked mad and ready to take it out on somebody, thought Clyde.

"I discovered that Peterson is away from his estate at the moment and is expected back Sunday. This is, in my view, good news as I feel that everyone will be more relaxed and less alert."

Everyone nodded their agreement. "We must assume that Peterson has eyes and ears everywhere," said Clyde. "If so, people will be reporting anything out of place to his henchmen, hoping to be valuable, so we must be discreet."

He stepped over to his bed, picked up a bundle of clothing and handed it to Rosalinda. She retired to her room to try the clothing on.

Jameson explained he had been successful; purchasing an older, enclosed wagon, complete with a harness for a horse and some items to put in it and hang on the sides. "It weren't hard to find a horse experienced at pulling a wagon. She's a mite old, but will suit."

"I was thinking," said Clyde, "would you be recognized from the auction? Did Peterson's men see you?"

Jameson thought for a moment. "I was standing near to Johnny, but I didn't talk to anyone. It seems doubtful they would remember me."

"Very well," said Clyde.

"I obtained some clothing and made sure they fit well enough," said Henry, quietly.

"Henry, you're really key to this plan. Do you think folks on the plantation will talk to you?"

"Depends on how scared they are," replied Henry, "but if they don't, I know who will."

Everyone looked at him. He reached in his pocket and held up a handful of hard candy. "The children," he said smiling. "They'll know if Johnny is there."

Rosalinda returned, wearing the nun's habit. She was transformed. As everyone stared at her, she smiled.

"You look like a nun; a beautiful one, but a nun," said Clyde and everyone chuckled.

Clyde told them what he had seen at the plantation and using the map he showed them his notes of where he had ridden, what he had seen and where there were houses. He mentioned the huge man he had seen.

"He was at the auction with Peterson and his man, a butler type," said Jameson.

"Yes," said Clyde. "It was the butler that I spoke to and I saw the large man. Might be the foreman."

Turning once again to the map, where Clyde had drawn in the great-house and the buildings he had seen, he made an x at a spot on a road at the opposite end of the estate. "It's over two miles from the far end of the estate to the great-house," he said. "We'll meet at a wagon yard, where Jameson has staged his wagon and horse and I have left the buggy and horse loaned to me. We'll leave late tomorrow afternoon, say half-past five, an hour or so before dark. Jameson, when you see Rosalinda and I depart, wait twenty minutes before you leave. I don't have to tell you to make sure no one sees Henry get in the back."

Jameson nodded and Clyde continued, "There's likely to be folks on the road, returning from town. You know what to say if you come across someone. We'll meet at the spot I've marked and hide."

Clyde paused and looked around the room. Everyone was listening intently. "Let's say two hours after dark, around eight-thirty, Rosalinda and I will leave the hiding place. Jameson, wait two minutes, then follow us. I will pass the drop off point, you'll know it, it's the biggest tree around. About a hundred feet past it, I'll stop, get out and pretend to check the horse's harness. You stop by the large tree and let Henry out and wait until we've turned around and passed you returning to the hiding place before you do the same. Henry, you'll have to work your way down to the double-row of cabins to try to find someone to talk to. You'll be able to stay in the trees for most of the way, but you'll have to cross a good quarter mile of cane stalks. They've been cut so they aren't tall. You have to stay low."

Henry nodded his understanding.

"We'll return to the hiding place and wait until a half-hour past midnight and then return to the same drop off positions. We will wait there until four-thirty. If you don't return, we'll come back at half-past midnight, Sunday night."

Clyde noted that everyone's faces were solemn. The strain they must be under, he thought.

Johnny realized he couldn't afford to sleep although he had been digging all night. It was Friday morning and if Peterson was planning to kill him on Sunday, he had to get out Saturday night if possible. It might be Sunday afternoon before they came for him, but his chances of escaping were so much greater in the dark and with a head start, before they could get the dogs after him. The metal piece of hoe helped tremendously, but the work was slow. Johnny was able to get into the hole he had dug, but he had little room to scrape at the dirt under the logs. He realized he needed to make the hole he was in deeper and that would take time. Weak and exhausted from lack of food, sunlight and worry for his family, he worked without stopping, pushing himself. All day Friday, he scratched at the dirt, gathered it on his tin plate and tossed it out of the hole.

Suddenly, Johnny awoke, confused, unsure of where he was, then he realized he had fallen asleep in the small hole he was trying to deepen. He sat for a moment, thinking. It didn't look like he would be able to dig himself out in time, although he would keep trying.

When they came for him, he could use the piece of a hoe as a weapon. He'd go down fighting and do his best to take some of them with him, but he'd wait his chance, try to get to Peterson.

Saturday morning, when the old man kneeled down and pushed his tin of food under the cell bars, the man studied Johnny's face and raising a thin arm, waved it around, pointing at the back of Johnny's cell, raising his eyebrows.

In his state of extreme fatigue, Johnny wasn't thinking clearly, but he suddenly understood and got up and walked to the back and pointed at the corner where he was digging the hole. In the dim light, Johnny could just see the old man nod as he got up holding Johnny's old plate, turn and leave. The door bolt slammed home and Johnny felt a surge of hope.

Saturday passed slowly for everyone as they waited to embark on what would hopefully be a successful rescue of Johnny. They had met for breakfast and Clyde had suggested they not meet for lunch, that everyone do whatever they needed to do, but he suggested everyone try to sleep a little in the afternoon.

When evening arrived, Jameson appeared at the wagon yard and paid up. The owner was surprised. "You leaving town this late?" he asked.

"No, no," replied Jameson. "Most of my personal stuff is at my friends. I'm going to load up and get an early start in the morning."

The man nodded uncertainly, but he'd been paid, so what folks did was none of his concern.

Henry, poorly dressed and a battered hat pulled low on his head, waited outside the wagon yard's fence, smoking his pipe. Clyde, dressed in a black frock, walked Rosalinda, dressed in her habit, complete with a veil, to the buggy and helped her into its seat, then went in search of the wagon yard's owner and his horse.

"Can I help you with the horse, Father?" asked the owner.

"No thank you my son, May God bless you," replied Clyde.

Reaching his buggy, Clyde harnessed the horse and seeing Jameson watching, nodded as he wiggled the reins and the horse started forward. Jameson pulled out his pocket watch and checked it. Jameson spent some time fussing with his gear and twenty minutes later, climbed up on the wagon seat and drove his rig around the wagon yard, stopping in the back to jump down and tug at the harness. When he climbed back into his seat and out the wagon yard's gates, Henry was in the back of the wagon.

The journey to the far reaches of the Peterson sugar plantation was uneventful. As expected they passed wagons, buggies and folks riding horses on the road. Some were traveling to New Orleans, others returning home. Seeing the priest and nun, people waved, but everyone ignored Jameson, the drummer, except for one elderly couple in a wagon who waved him over and asked about an axe.

He had one in the back and reached in through the flap covering it, saying "It's just here," and Henry handed it to him. He sold it and hurried on his way. Later that evening, when they were all well-hidden off the road, in the trees, Henry asked, "Why didn't you tell them folks you didn't have an axe?"

"Why, it never occurred to me, I'm a drummer at the moment, after all," said Jameson, quite serious.

Quiet laughter broke the tension they were all feeling.

By nine o'clock that night, Henry was standing behind a tree, studying the area. Not long after, Clyde, Rosalinda and Jameson were back at their staging area, sitting quietly, wrapped in blankets, watching the moon and praying for Johnny and Henry.

Chapter 35

Caleb was relieved of his kitchen duties and assigned to tend to the horses. B.R. went back to wrangling longhorns and taming horses. They saw each other nightly, but both were subdued and several hands noticed they weren't themselves.

One day, out on the range, as B.R. and a fellow cowboy sat their horses, smoking, the man said, "We've all noticed you and Caleb ain't been up to your usual hijinks lately."

B. R. didn't respond and the cowboy didn't speak again. When they had finished their smokes, B.R. said, "Yeah, we both got women on our mind."

The cowboy and Billy Ray looked at each other. The cowboy nodded, as though to indicate this explained everything and the two pressed their horses forward.

Saturday night, as Clyde, Rosalinda, Jameson and Henry rode out of the wagon yard in New Orleans, B.R. was entering the Café del Rio and Caleb, his cane beside him on the seat, was driving the Circle C's small buggy through the streets of San Antonio, on his way to pick up Mollie for supper. Both men had spent some time getting ready. They had blacked their boots and brushed their hats. Both were wearing their best outfits. A considerable amount of *Rowland's Macassar Oil* had been applied to their hair, which they had brushed carefully before putting on their hats.

A fellow who served as the ranch barber, trimmed B.R.'s beard and mustache.

"Woo-wee!" declared one cowboy. "You two are gonna draw some attention. What kind I can't say, cause you look like a couple of New York dandies!"

This brought considerable laugher from everyone in the bunkhouse, although they were all trying to look their best for the Saturday night trip to town.

Caleb and B.R. stopped at the edge of town, B.R. bringing his horse up beside the buggy. "Good luck to you," said Caleb, smiling.

"Just a second cowboy," replied B.R. dismounting and stepping around to the buggy. "A while back I bought this." He held out a small bottle. "I reckon now's the time for us to use it, but I weren't in no mood to take no guff off the fellows."

Caleb took the bottle and studied the label, *Yardley's English Lavender.* Caleb smiled.

"Well go ahead, splash some on. It can't hurt and Lord knows we need all the help we can get."

Mollie's hair was curled and she was wearing a long dress and a hat. Caleb thought her so beautiful, he couldn't speak. "Aren't you going to say something, like hello?" asked Mollie.

Billy Ray stood in the door of the Café del Rio, holding his hat as he watched Topsannah wait on a customer. She turned, saw him and her face lit up. Her beautiful smile seemed to fill the room and B.R. thought for one terrible moment he might pass out as he felt a weakness pass through him and then he took a deep breath and smiled back at her.

CHAPTER 36

Not long after dark, Johnny, who had been digging all day, stretched out on the ground to relive the pain in his legs and back. He quickly fell asleep. When he awoke, some two hours later, he climbed back into the hole and was startled to hear noises outside. He listened. Someone was digging. He felt a wave of emotion surge through his body. There was hope.

Henry wasted no time moving to the rows of cabins. Smoke rose from most of them. He was unarmed, a situation that had been debated at length. Finally he agreed that were he stopped, he might be able to pass himself off as one of the blacks living on the plantation, but if he was searched and a weapon found, he'd be killed for sure.

He stopped at the first cabin, listened for a moment, and then knocked softly. A thin black man opened the door a crack and studied Henry Bear. "I don't know you," said the man. "What you want?"

"I'm looking for a white man. Held prisoner."

After a moment, the man shut the door without speaking. There was another door at the end of the porch, so Henry knocked on it. A black woman opened it and looked at him, frowning.

"What you want Negro?" she asked suspiciously. "I think you knocked at the wrong door. You looking for Sheba, she on the row in front." With that, she shut the door.

Henry tried a third door and although smoke came from the chimney, no one answered his knock. At the fourth door, a man listened to Henry's question and replied, "Don't know nothing about no prisoner. Only white men hereabouts is the bosses."

At the fifth door, Henry decided to try a different question. When the door cracked open, he couldn't see anything, but the whites of someone's eyes. "Sorry to be a bother this late," he said, "Could you tell me where the stockade be? I think my friend be put there."

"How you not know where it at?" asked a female voice. "If you trying to get in my house, you better think again. I'll lay you out with a frying pan quicker you can kill a chicken."

"Sister, I mean no harm. Can you tell me?"

After a few seconds of hesitating, the woman said, "Fool, it a good half-mile behind the outhouses, in the trees back there. Don't know what good it'll do you." With that, she shut the door.

Henry smiled.

Two black men, using shovels were sweating in the cold night air, as they worked to dig under the wall where Johnny was scraping away. When their shovels broke through, Johnny climbed out of the hole and began scooping earth up with his tin plate. Soon, the hole was big enough and he climbed into the hole, under the log wall and up the other side, where the men grabbed his arms and pulled him free.

The three stood looking at each other for a minute. "Thank you," said Johnny.

"We can't hide you," said one of the men. When they come for you and you're gone, they will search everywhere. Lord Peterson has dogs and he like to run 'em. You best git." The man pointed east and Johnny nodded.

"You folks know slavery is against the law now?"

"We heard, but what can we do? Some tried to leave and they beat or killed."

The men disappeared into the darkness and Johnny began walking east. Someone will pay for a terrible price for helping me escape, he thought, but before I'm finished with this, justice will be done.

The two men were startled when they noticed someone coming toward them in the dark. They hid and were very surprised to see a big black man picking his way through the trees. They looked at each other. Seeing him in the moonlight, the two men looked at each other. Henry was big and they certainly didn't recognize him.

One of the men placed his shovel on the ground and approached Henry while the other man, holding his shovel high, as a weapon, melted into the darkness.

"Big man, what you doing out here?" asked the man, walking toward Henry.

Henry was relieved it was a black man confronting him, but he knew that often some slaves curried favor by reporting to whites.

Henry didn't respond, but stood still, waiting. The man reached him, stopped and stared. "I don't know you," said the man.

Henry smiled. "I'm new," he said, "got lost looking for the outhouse."

As the second man crept up behind Henry, shovel at the ready, the first man responded. "New are you. What's the foreman's name?"

"I don't recall he saying," replied Henry.

The man held up his hand and the man behind Henry stopped. "He always say. Want us Negroes to know. What you doing out here?"

Sighing, Henry said, "I'm looking for a white man. Told he might be out here somewhere in the stockade."

Johnny worked his way through the trees, wondering how long it was until first light. He was weak and soon he felt exhausted. Stopping to rest for a moment, he thought he heard his name. He listened. If he didn't know better, he'd a thought it was Henry calling to him. There, he heard it again. "I'm here," he said and waited. In a moment, he saw a smiling Henry Bear staring at him.

"Am I dreaming?" he asked the figure.

Henry stepped close and grabbed Johnny in a bear hug. "I come to rescue you, but it don't look like you need my help," said Henry, stepping back, "but no time to talk, we need to get out of here afore light."

Henrietta was a twenty-year-old black girl, who had been a house servant before the old woman in charge had noticed her talking to Lord Peterson one day and had sent her back to the cabins and the sugarcane fields.

"You getting above yourself," the old woman had said.

Henrietta was outside smoking when she saw two black men with shovels walk by. What could they be up to this time of night, she wondered? They didn't see her as she put out her smoke and followed them; all the way to the stockade where, it was said, a white man was being held. Seeing a chance to win favor and return to service at the great-house, she ran. Mr. Jackson, the foreman had his own room with an outside door in the bunkhouse not far from the stables. She would tell him.

When Jackson opened the door, his face was enraged, but Henrietta talked fast. "What's your name woman?" he asked. She told him and he told her to get back to her cabin.

Twenty minutes later, he and nine men were dressed, mounted, armed and riding. Jackson had given a moment of thought to the dogs, but Lord Peterson didn't like anyone but himself running them, so he decided against taking them. The escaped white man would head east for the trees was his best guess, but he sent two men west and two north to be sure. All had orders not to kill the man, but he warned them, if he got away, somebody would take his place.

Henry and Johnny walked and stumbled east. It was dark in the trees and Johnny was exhausted and weak from his ordeal and lack of sleep. Finally, they stumbled on what appeared to be an old, unused road. Weeds and dead grass covered it, but the lack of trees and deep ruts revealed its former use.

They took to the road, but weren't on it long when a horse and rider appeared in the darkness. "Don't bother running. I got you dead to rights with a Henry."

After both men had been put in irons, on both hands and legs, Jackson climbed down off his horse and beat them while his men watched and cheered him on.

Henry kept grinning at Jackson and Johnny said, "Only a coward, would beat a man in chains."

This sent Jackson into a fury and he redoubled his efforts. Finally, exhausted, Jackson yelled for the two men to be put in the stockade. They were dragged into the cell beside the one formerly occupied by Johnny and left there. The barred door slamming shut and the bolt clanging as it was sent home.

CHAPTER 37

The group sat at the pickup-site, silent, listening, grim-faced. When Clyde announced it was four-thirty, in the same breath, he said, "We can wait till five, then we'll have to go."

The journey back to New Orleans was a torment. No one spoke, but in their minds, everyone was thinking the worst. They would likely never see Johnny or Henry again. Clyde expected to see Rosalinda cry, but she didn't. She sat rigid and grim-faced on the seat beside him.

When they reached New Orleans, they went to a different wagon yard and made arrangements for the horses, wagon and buggy, pretending not to know each other.

Outside the wagon yard, Clyde said, "We must get some sleep."

At the hotel St. James, Jameson asked Clyde, "What if, you know, they ain't there tonight?"

Clyde replied, "We'll have to discuss it." With that, he turned and walked away.

In the dark cell, Henry updated Johnny, who, hearing that Rosalinda had insisted on coming, was distressed, but Henry said, "I'd like to see you tell her she couldn't come."

In spite of his fatigue, pain and worry, Johnny smiled.

"What do you reckon will happen, when we don't show up tonight?" asked Henry.

Quietly, Johnny said, "Some folks would hire a lawyer, try to negotiate our release. Maybe try to get a federal judge to issue a search warrant. Rosalinda will know that time is important and she'll tell Clyde and Jameson, 'the law be damned.' Likely she'll want to come for us."

The door to the stockade banged open just after noon. After they were dragged out of the stockade, the chains were removed, but Johnny and Henry were surrounded by six men on horseback. One of the men said, "Follow me," and started his horse toward the great-house, as the other men took positions to the sides and back.

Johnny and Henry were grabbed by the arms and taken into the great-house through a back door and taken to what Johnny identified as Peterson's study. Inside stood Jackson, a large revolver hanging on his side, scowling at them. He nodded his head and the two men who had escorted them in let go of them and walked out. "You," he said forcefully to Johnny. "Move to the center of the room and take your hat off."

Johnny moved to the center of the room, but didn't remove his hat. Jackson, his face angry, walked up behind him and knocked the hat from his head. Johnny could see a very large chair sitting on a raised platform at the back of the room.

After a few minutes, Peterson, dressed again in a suit, entered through a door at the back of the room, hatless, walked to the chair and sat in it. "Approach," he said to Johnny.

Johnny walked forward, stopping about ten feet from Peterson, who sat, studying him. "I'm told your name is Johnny Black and you are from Texas. Is that correct?"

Staring at Peterson, Johnny replied, "It is."

Looking over Johnny's head at Henry, standing in the back of the room where Jackson stood watch, Peterson asked, "Is this your manservant?"

"No," said Johnny flatly. "He's my ranch foreman."

Peterson's face showed surprise. "Oh my," he said, smiling. "I am a French nobleman, a Marquis. My family name is Beausoleil." Seeing Johnny frown, he continued, "You know me as Lord Peterson. My family name was made more English when some of my ancestors settled in England, but I spent my life in France, until I came here to take over the plantation."

Johnny didn't respond. Peterson seemed lost in thought, then he continued, "I'm sure you know why you're here. Warnings were afforded you a number of times that I wished to purchase the large horses and you ignored those warnings, as you can see, at your peril."

Johnny stood silent, staring at Peterson.

"I am sure you regret your actions, but, you have disrespected me and I must have satisfaction. To that end, I have decided we shall duel. It is customary for the challenged party to choose the weapons, but I, doubtful of your adherence to the rules, have made the decision for you. You see, I am afraid if we provide you with a loaded pistol, you might choose to try and shoot me outright. Oui? We shall fight with swords. As I prefer a bit of action, we'll put it off for a few days to give you a chance to rest and recover from your recent adventures."

Johnny continued to stare silently at Peterson.

"I think it only fair to tell you, Mr. Black, I am a fencing master. In France I am held in very high regard for my skills. I have available epees, foils and sabers, but I think we shall fight with sabers." He smiled.

"Mr. Jackson, please see that these two men have blankets, and all the food and water they wish. I want no further harm to them as I need Mr. Black in top form for our engagement and his man can attend him."

He stood, then turned to look once again at Johnny. "I think three days should suffice. We shall meet on the hill to the south of the house at daybreak on Wednesday. Oh, and Mr. Black, it shall be a fight to the death. If Mr. Jackson agrees, we shall let your man-servant live and work on the plantation after the engagement is concluded. He's big. He'll make a fine slave."

Monday morning, arising from another night of fitful sleep, Rosalinda, Clyde and Jameson had breakfast in the hotel, although Rosalinda ate very little. Clyde discussed engaging an attorney and trying to get a search warrant, but his heart wasn't in it.

As the plates were cleared, the three sat with coffee and Rosalinda said, "We must confront this man. If the parish sheriff is on his side and he has powerful friends, it is the only way. Johnny once said, 'if you must fight, it is often best to get right to it'."

"Rosalinda," said Clyde, "you've Lucrecia to think about. Why don't you go home and let Jameson and I deal with it?"

"No," she said, firmly.

Shaking his head in resignation, Clyde replied, "I've given this possibility some thought. There are always men about such as we need. It will require cash; perhaps a good deal of it."

A few hours later, Rosalinda had telegraphed the bank she and Johnny used in San Antonio and arrangements had been made with a bank in New Orleans for her to obtain funds. Clyde made a trip to the Orleans parish sheriff's office. Jameson spent the morning making the rounds of saloons, talking to barkeeps and owners, exchanging money for information.

As agreed, the three met again, in Clyde's room. The mood was somber.

"I can draw whatever funds are required," said Rosalinda.

"I met with the Orleans parish sheriff," said Clyde, who was quiet for a moment and then continued, "I made up a story about being in the area, looking for a wanted man and told him, in conversation, I had heard rumors about the Peterson Sugar Plantation and was curious about it. He told me what we already knew. The man has connections to the state government and is friends with the sheriff in his parish. That said, I think we all understand we'll get no help from the state law, however, there are federal troops present here, in New Orleans."

"Will they help?" asked Rosalinda, her voice hopeful.

"I'm going to visit the Commanding Officer this afternoon," said Clyde.

After a moment, Jameson said, "I pray you'll be successful, but if not, I am to meet with a man who might prove useful."

Clyde and Rosalinda looked at Jameson with questioning eyes.

Jameson stroked his beard and said, "One of the barkeeps gave me a name. Through an intermediary I was able to arrange a meeting. It seems the man doesn't live in the area, but he's about. We meet tonight."

"Jameson," said Clyde, "if my meeting with the Commander is successful, I'll stop by your room and let you know. If I'm not successful, I'll accompany you and carry the funds."

Clyde looked at Rosalinda, who nodded her approval. "Shall we all meet tonight?" asked Clyde, looking at Rosalinda.

"Yes, please, I shouldn't sleep otherwise," said Rosalinda and Clyde nodded.

"Here at ten, if that suits."

CHAPTER 38

When B.R. had finished his meal and Topsannah brought him peach cobbler and fresh coffee, the café was almost empty. He seized the opportunity. "Topsannah, my boss, Mr. Christie, well, we're having a barn dance next Saturday night. Will you come with me?"

Surprised, Topsannah hesitated, then said, "I must work."

"Could someone work in your place? There was a woman helping here last week."

Topsannah looked at him. "My father-in-law is very thankful for your help. I will ask him."

Billy Ray couldn't speak, so he just smiled and nodded.

A few minutes later a smiling Topsannah returned and said, "Yes, I will accompany you to the dance."

"Yee-haaa!" yelled B.R. throwing his hat into the air. The café had two tables of customers and they all looked over in alarm at the cowboy who had yelled and thrown his hat into the air.

Shaking her head in disbelief, Topsannah walked away to tend to the other customers.

Mollie and Caleb had supper and were walking the streets of San Antonio, talking.

"Caleb, is something on your mind?" asked Mollie.

Caleb, walking better, but still using his cane, stopped, looked at her, smiled and said, " Mollie, I'm right taken with you and well, you'll be going home soon."

"Yes, I must return home. I'm the only child and my mother is alone. She could use my help. I thought you were going to California."

"Ah, yep, that's right, but well, dang it, Mollie, I'd like to see more of you, but my friend Billy Ray said something made me think."

Mollie stood, looking at him. A man eased past them.

Continuing, Caleb said, "I'm a cowhand, a buckaroo. I earn forty dollars a month. You're well, you are a banker's daughter and I can tell, you've been to school. B.R., that's what we call Billy Ray most times, he was saying I don't have anything to offer you and that's a gospel truth."

Smiling, Mollie replied, "My, you are very observant buckaroo. Yes, I graduated from The Columbia Female Baptist Academy in Columbia, Missouri. Does that bother you?"

"No, but I can't support you, well, like you're accustomed to."

"Caleb, why don't you come home with me. I'm sure mother can help you get a job in a bank. You'll made twice as much money and as you learn banking you can work your way up."

Caleb stared at her. "Work inside. In a bank?"

"Why sure, you're smart, you'll catch on quick. We can pick out some suitable clothes for you and before you know it you'll be a regular gentleman."

Stunned at the thought, Caleb smiled a weak smile and responded, "Sure, now that'd be something."

The couple continued their walk, Mollie telling Caleb about Missouri while he nodded and smiled, trying not to think about being confined inside a bank on a regular basis.

Caleb took Mollie home and on the doorstep asked her to the barn dance the following Saturday night. She agreed, but said she would be leaving for Missouri the following Monday.

He took the buggy to the stable where B.R. had left his horse and walked to the Grand Saloon.

B.R. was waiting on him, nursing a whiskey. The moment Caleb saw him, he knew it had gone well.

After purchasing a whiskey at the bar, Caleb joined B.R. at his table. Neither man spoke. Caleb lifted his glass in a toast and B.R. lifted his. The two took a drink.

"I see things went your way," said Caleb.

"What makes you think that?" inquired B.R. "I haven't said a word."

"Ha," replied Caleb. "Anybody within a half-mile could see you're either happy drunk or suffering from a bad case of calico fever!"

Smiling, Billy Ray replied, "She's coming to the barn dance on Saturday night. I'm to pick her up at her house at five sharp, just like we talked about. We pick up Mollie and we'll be back to the ranch in time to eat before the dancing starts."

"Well, how about that! I'm thinking it was that English Lavender what did the trick."

"Could a been," replied B.R., "but I don't care what it was. She smiled at me and she's coming to the dance with me." Suddenly looking serious, B.R. said, "What about Mollie?"

"Oh, she's coming," said Caleb. "I'm to pick her up at a quarter past five, like we agreed, so I'm thinking we did good."

B.R. held his glass up and said, "To success and Yardley's English Lavender."

Caleb touched his glass to B.R.'s and the two drank.

The two sat a minute and B.R. said, "You look like your tail is dragging a mite."

Caleb didn't respond for several minutes and B.R. didn't press the issue. Finally, Caleb said, "I thought about what you said and you're right, so I spoke to Mollie about it."

"She has some thoughts on the subject?"

"Yep, she wants me to come to Missouri with her."

Billy Ray nodded, sipped his whiskey and said, "I expected she'd want to return to her family. I been bracing myself; thinking of you leaving."

"She wants me to work in a bank."

Billy Ray looked at Caleb, his face expressing his surprise. "Work in a bank?"

"Yep."

"Dang."

"Yep."

"We ought to turn in, head home early in the morning so we can help with sorting out the barn for the dance. We won't have a lot of time during the week."

"Yep."

Chapter 39

At half past seven, Clyde and Jameson left the hotel and walked to the French Quarter. Reaching the entrance to a dark alleyway, hardly large enough for two men to walk side by side, Jameson hesitated. Here in the French Quarter the gas lamps provided enough light to see fairly well, but he would open to attack in the dark alley. He had a revolver stuck in his waist under his coat and a knife in his boot, but if he was attacked he wouldn't have time to use them.

Suddenly, nodding to Clyde, he stepped into the dark and began walking, counting his steps. As he counted sixty, he came to a door and he knocked on it three times. It opened and he said, "Jefferson Davis," a password that caused him pause, and was admitted, but when he asked for 'Gator' he was searched and his gun and knife taken from him. It was dark in the room, but there were several lit oil lamps and Jameson could see a bar, tables and people. He was taken to a table in the back corner of the small room and as he took a seat and his eyes adjusted to the darkness, he saw a long-haired, heavily bearded man sitting across from him pouring whiskey from a bottle into a glass. Out of the darkness, an arm reached down and set an empty glass in front of Jameson and the man across from him reached across the table and filled it.

After a moment, a deep voice asked, "Do you have something for me?"

Jameson reached into his greatcoat pocket and pulling his hand out, placed a ten-dollar gold piece on the table and pushed it across to the man. The cost of the meeting.

Taking the coin, the man asked, "What can I do for you?"

"I'm in need of some men to rescue two people. It won't be a lawful intervention and there's likely to be gunplay."

"It's possible I might be able to help you," said Gator, "how many fighting men are there holding these folks?"

"Hard to say. At least ten and could be as many as twenty."

"So far, I don't see a problem. Tell me more."

Jameson told Gator about Peterson, the plantation and the fact they were certain he was keeping the blacks working for him as slaves.

Across the table, in the dim light cast by the oil lamps, Jameson could see Gator expose rotten teeth in what Jameson thought must be a smile.

"That's interesting," said Gator. "My friends and I are all former Confederate soldiers."

Jameson felt a queasy feeling in his stomach as he digested this information.

Gator gave Jameson a minute, then continued, "I see you're surprised. Don't let it concern you none, I ain't never had no slave and I sure as hell didn't fight for slavery. I fought cause I was told them Yankees was coming down here to take over and I don't cotton to foreigners telling me what to do. Now it's come true. Them northern types, the Republicans, is running things in this state and there are Yankee soldiers at the state house."

Jameson nodded, relief flooding his body.

"We're swamp people, me and mine. We live free in the bayous and bald cypress swamps; fishing, trapping and hunting. That said, we do require cash money from time to time. We have our standards mind you; we don't take from poor folk, and we don't kill unless we're threatened, but this fellow seems like somebody I wouldn't cotton to. How soon we talking?"

"As quick as arrangements can be made," replied Jameson.

"I reckon I'll need say, six men besides myself. Now, I learned in my time fighting them Billy Yanks, that things don't always go like you plan so keeping something in reserve is smart thinking, you follow me?"

"Yes," said Clyde, wondering what the man was getting to.

"What I'm thinking is I'll bring along the cavalry and hold it in reserve, just in case."

Clyde visualized thirty men on horseback and wondered what that would cost.

Talking out loud to himself, Gator mumbled, "Eight men at fifty dollar per man."

Pausing, looking at Jameson like he'd never seen him before, Gator said, "It'll cost you one thousand dollars. Five hundred afore I so much as give it another thought and five hundred when we meet at this plantation. That includes my men, myself, the cavalry and expenses." Gator's face broke into a huge smile.

Jameson stared at the man. "Mr. Gator, sir, that's an awful lot of money. What expenses are you referring to?"

"Cartridges and the like," replied Gator, his face serious. "Oh, I forgot, I don't take paper money. Gold. Payment in gold."

Jameson sipped his whiskey. Gator sipped his whiskey. The two men looked at each other.

"I need a few minutes to confer with my associate," said Jameson.

Gator nodded and Jameson rose and left the saloon, returning to the street where Clyde waited.

"He appears capable, but he wants one thousand dollars; five hundred now, in gold."

"I'll need some light, built a smoke," replied Clyde.

Jameson rolled a quirly and turning to the wall, struck a match. After lighting his smoke, he held it as Clyde, also facing the wall, pulled a bag from his greatcoat and removed gold coins from the bag and put them in his pocket, before handing Jameson the bag.

"There's five hundred in gold coins in the bag."

Jameson gave him a questioning look and Clyde said, "I brought eight hundred."

Returning to the saloon, Jameson found Gator and paid him.

"Down to business," said Gator, his tone suddenly very serious. "You have a map?"

Jameson pulled the map that Clyde had drawn on from his pocket and Gator pulled the lamp closer. The two men bent over the map and began to talk in low tones. Gator raised his voice just a little once. "You understand, nothing will go according to plan. It never does."

Wednesday morning, long before daybreak, three travelers, leading two saddled horses, make their way out of Orleans parish. Anyone passing them would have said they passed three men, but in fact the three included Jameson, Clyde and Rosalinda, who was wearing pants and a man's hat. Johnny's revolver was in the saddlebags on one of the rented horses and his rifle slung in a scabbard attached to the saddle. All three were praying they would find Johnny and Henry alive, but if not, they would use the horses to carry their bodies.

They had paid out of the hotel and Clyde had booked passage for five people on a ship leaving that afternoon, heading to Galveston. Clyde, a man of experience in planning, had mentioned a cough and inquired after a local doctor and had been informed one was located close to their hotel. He asked for and was given the address. Just in case.

A mile from the Peterson Sugar Plantation, a bit off the main road, the three found a small group of men sitting around a fire, drinking coffee. Hobbled horses were grazing and a small wagon sat with a tarpaulin thrown over its cargo.

Jameson counted nine men, including Gator. He guessed the 'cavalry' was waiting somewhere else. I'd hate to be on the bad side of this crew, he thought, studying the men, who, in a world of rough appearing men, were in a class unto themselves.

"Morning," said Gator to Jameson, ignoring the other two. "You got something for me?"

Jameson pulled a bag from his greatcoat and handed it to Gator.

"Somebody fetch these folks some coffee!" exclaimed Gator, and two men jumped up to see to it.

As Jameson, Rosalinda and Clyde sipped their coffee, Jameson said to the other two, "If we get in close, we might have to fight. Best to remember these people are all a party to keeping folks as slaves, nine years after it was made illegal. Peterson is pure evil and he and those helping him are evildoers. Don't hesitate if you're confronted. They aren't going to show you any mercy."

A good hour before daybreak, Johnny and Henry were taken from the stockade and marched to the servant's quarters, where they were allowed to wash up at a basin and were fed breakfast with coffee, while the two white men, holding revolvers, stood against the wall and watched them carefully.

Johnny's beard was full and he was gaunt. His clothes were filthy from his digging and imprisonment. He was still sore and his face bruised from being beaten by Jackson while his hands and feet were chained. Below Henry's left eye lay a large, deep open wound, still seeping. Had it been stitched shut, it would have healed quick enough, but as it was, it looked worrisome to Johnny. Henry also had a large lump on his forehead.

"What the hell is a saber?" asked Henry.

"It's a kind of French sword," replied Johnny as he ate.

"Do you know anything about this fencing stuff he was talking about?"

"No, but I served with a Frenchman for a while during the war. He had a French sword called a 'foil', it's a bit different, but he was always jumping around pretending to fight somebody, told me he was 'fencing'. I studied him some."

Henry looked up from his meal and studied Johnny. "You know I ain't never gonna be a slave again, so if they kill you they gonna have to kill me. Fact of the matter is, if I get any kind of chance, I'll be taking Mr. Jackson with me."

"I'm thinking if things don't go Peterson's way, Jackson will shoot me, so we have to consider that."

"That makes me feel some better, like you thinking you got a chance against this 'fencing master', ain't that what he called himself?"

Johnny smiled. "Yep.

"You got a plan?"

"Well, I served with the cavalry for a while, in the war, so I've swung a sword, but no, I don't have a plan. You 'member, me telling you about the book, *The Art of War*?"

"I do."

"Well, that Frenchman and me discussed it a good bit. It says something like 'if you know yourself and you know your enemy, you don't need to fear a battle,' or something like that. I know myself and I know a bit about men and fighting, so I figure the man's making a mistake, handing me a weapon."

At dawn, the men took Johnny and Henry to the hill and they waited. A half-hour later, Peterson appeared, and Jackson, carrying two swords and wearing a revolver on his hip followed a few steps behind him.

Looking at the two guards who had walked Johnny and Henry to the hill, Peterson said, "Send those two men to their breakfast."

Jackson waved them away, as he and Peterson walked up to where Johnny and Henry stood.

Peterson said, "Mr. Black, good morning. After we remove our coats, you will have your choice of sabers. We will move away and face each other at ten paces. At my command, the duel to the death, shall commence."

CHAPTER 40

Music rang out in the barn on the Circle C as people danced, drank, laughed and talked. Topsannah and Mollie were in great demand. Both looked wonderful in colorful dresses and Billy Ray and Caleb fumed as they watched them dance with other men, but a wonderful time was had by all.

Caleb commandeered the small buggy to take Mollie home. He planned to talk to her and didn't want an audience. Someone had taken the big buggy, so B.R. and Topsannah drove into San Antonio in the supply wagon. Topsannah was sitting close to B.R. and holding on to his arm. As the wagon maneuvered a curve in the road, they encountered a large deer standing in the road. The buck studied them and then ambled into the trees. Laughing, Topsannah turned her head and looked at Billy Ray and at that moment, he knew for a fact that he had found the girl he had been searching for.

Smiling at her, B.R. said, "I was looking for you down in Mexico, and you were here in San Antonio, the whole time."

As the buggy rolled through the time, Caleb tried to gather his courage. Finally, he said, "Mollie, I sure had a fine time tonight."

"I had a wonderful time, thank you for bringing me."

"Mollie, I know you gotta go home, your momma and all, but see, I care for you, a lot. I do. But I won't be going to Missouri with you."

Mollie turned quickly in her seat. "Why not? Is something wrong?"

"No, nothing is wrong, I just can't go."

"Is there another girl, Caleb? Tell me, I'd rather know."

"Of course not. I told you I got feelings for you. It's just, well, I just can't go and that's that."

"Fine," said Mollie, her body stiffening. "If you think I'll stay you are wrong. I told you, my mother needs me and I'm leaving on the stage on Monday."

"I know you're going," said Caleb. "I hope you have a safe journey."

They rode in silence until they came to the house where Mollie had rented a room. Caleb helped her down.

"It was nice to meet you Caleb."

"It was nice to meet you Mollie."

Waiting on the stage, Mollie felt sure Caleb would appear, his valise in hand, but she was disappointed. Even as the stage rolled out toward Austin, she was looking out the window, to no avail. All the way to Missouri, she found herself crying one minute and so angry the next she wanted to break something. It took over two weeks to make the nine-hundred-mile trip back to Columbia where Mollie, after a brief welcome and reunion, burst into tears and confided in her mother.

"I heard nothing about an attempt to rob the bank," Mollie told her mother.

"Don't worry yourself with that child," replied her mother, "but what about this young man."

"He's a cad!" exclaimed Mollie.

Smiling, her mother responded, "Nevertheless, you seem taken with him."

"I love him mother, but I misjudged his feelings. I thought he loved me, but obviously, he doesn't."

"You said he worked on a ranch, is that right? What does he do on the ranch?"

"Oh, he's a forty-dollar a month cowboy. He said he didn't earn enough money to take care of me proper and I told him you would help him get a job in a bank."

Mollie's mother's eyebrows rose, then she smiled. "Dear, I think perhaps I see the reason the young man didn't come."

"What do you mean? How could you?"

"Sweetheart, you can't tame men. You have to let them be themselves."

"Mother, whatever are you talking about?" responded Mollie.

"That man wouldn't last a day clerking in a bank or working in a store. He's got to be outside, working with his hands, staying busy and coming in tired at the end of the day. It's the way of men like that."

"How would you know a thing like that?" asked Mollie.

"We both know a man like that, do we not?"

Mollie thought for a moment and exclaimed, "Uncle Ned!"

"Can you imagine my brother, Ned working in the bank?"

Mollie laughed and her mother joined in.

"The bank would fold in a week if he was working there," said Mollie's mother.

Mollie said, "We'd have to hogtie him to get him there," and she and her mother began to laugh again.

"Oh my, what was I thinking?" asked Mollie.

"You weren't," replied her mother. "You're in love. Did you tell him, what's his name, Caleb, I think you said, did you tell Caleb you inherited a good deal of money when your father was killed?"

"No, I didn't want him to know I have money, I had to make sure he loves me for me, not for my money."

"Dear, how do you feel about living on a ranch? Perhaps you should buy one. You could talk to Ned about it, but a large one I think." Her mother smiled.

"Oh mother, you're so wonderful," replied Mollie. "I'm going to send a telegram and have it taken out to the ranch he works on. I'll tell him my uncle Ned has a job for him on his ranch and we'll be able to see each other often."

"What if he doesn't come?" asked her mother.

Smiling, Mollie said, "I think he will."

B.R. and Caleb were working with a crew, branding longhorns in the cold January air. B.R. didn't bother trying to talk to Caleb. After Mollie left, Caleb had fallen into a melancholy that B.R. couldn't seem to pierce.

"I'm happy for you and Topsannah," Caleb had told B.R.

That was the last complete sentence he had spoken since the night of the dance. He answered questions with a shake of his head or a yes or no. Often, he didn't respond at all.

As the day grew late, the crew finished the last longhorn, put out the fire and mounted up. Nobody wanted to miss supper.

The evening meal was almost done, when a boy walked in with a telegram for Caleb. Surprised, Caleb dug out four-bits for the lad and tore open the message. He read it twice, his face somber. After the second reading he looked across the table at Billy Ray.

Caleb tried to speak calmly, but his face broke into a huge smile and he said, "B.R., if Mr. Christie will stand-still for it, this cowboy is riding for Missouri at first light!"

CHAPTER 41

Johnny took off his greatcoat and handed it to Henry. He walked over to Jackson and took a saber and walked into the middle of the small hill. Peterson watched him and then handed his coat to Jackson and took the other sword, whipping it through the air as he took his place, ten paces from Johnny.

Standing still, Johnny felt the weight of the saber and swung it through the air a few times. It was light, straight and had both a sharp point and a cutting edge. Not that different from the cavalry sword he had wielded for a year or more during his service with the cavalry during the war.

Looking up, Johnny saw Peterson in a stance with his left hand on his hip and his right holding his saber out in front of him. Suddenly Peterson yelled, "En Gärde!" as he advanced toward Johnny in a manner that made Johnny think of a prancing horse.

As he closed on Johnny, he suddenly lunged, trying to stab Johnny in the chest, but Johnny parried with his saber. In the blink of an eye, Peterson, his saber knocked downward by Johnny's parry, whipped it left and up, cutting a quarter-inch deep, three-inch-long, gash, in Johnny's face from the corner of his mouth up to his eye on the right side of his face.

As Peterson's sword went high after cutting Johnny's face, Johnny took advantage and stabbed his sword into Peterson. He went for the heart, but Peterson twisted and the blade entered his left shoulder, sinking deep, before Johnny pulled it out.

Two miles away, at the far end of the Peterson Sugar Plantation, an explosion rocked the air.

All six men on duty spurred their horses, headed for the site of the explosion. It had been set off by two of Gator's men, using dynamite.

At the same moment, four other men were setting up close to the stables where they had a view of the bunkhouse where the remaining guards were having their breakfast. Hearing the explosion, the men in the bunkhouse came out to look.

The six men riding to the site of the explosion gathered together, trying to figure out what had happened. Suddenly, their chatter was interrupted by a voice that rang out from the trees.

"We got you covered all the way to Sunday. Drop them rifles and gun belts afore we cut you down like a bunch of chicken-livered Yankees."

The six men were all former Confederate soldiers, all never-do-wells, but experienced in battle. As one, they opened fire into the trees as they turned their horses. Return fire hit one man and he fell forward out of his saddle and hit the ground, as his horse continued to run. The slaves were having their breakfast and hearing the explosion, looked out their doors, but stayed inside. They watched as the horsemen, fearing an attack on the great-house, thundered past. All the blacks closed their doors. This wasn't any of their affair.

Gator had sent two men with dynamite to create a diversion and draw out any guards in the fields. He sent four men to surround the bunkhouse where the men off duty were having breakfast. Two of his men drove the wagon down the road and stopped, facing the great-house.

Rosalinda, Jameson and Clyde rode behind Gator, leading the two extra horses. When the wagon stopped, Gator turned and indicated they should tie the extra horses to the trees on the side of the road. After they did so, the four of them rode their horses at a walk, toward the house.

Johnny, Peterson, Jackson and Henry all heard the explosion, but the life and death struggle they were involved in demanded their attention. After Peterson slashed Johnny's face and Johnny pierced Peterson's shoulder, Peterson backed away, a look of disbelief on his face. His left arm hung limp by his side. Johnny felt no pain, but he could feel the warm blood that had now begun to flow down his face. As was his way, Johnny charged. Peterson was caught off guard and quickly backed up even as he warded off the blows from Johnny's saber. Left, right, left, right, Johnny slashed as Peterson backed, parrying the blows.

Finally, Peterson completed a move and his saber sank into Johnny's left thigh, but Peterson paid a price as Johnny swung his saber cutting a bloody gash across Peterson's forehead and then stabbing Peterson, the blade running completely through his neck, but missing the major arteries.

Peterson stepped back several paces, but Johnny, in spite of his leg wound, started toward Peterson again.

Peterson suddenly yelled, "You're a mad man! Jackson! I am leaving the field. Kill both of them."

Johnny was only a step away and Peterson, dropping his saber, his left arm hanging loosely, used his right to staunch the blood flowing from his neck wound as he turned and began stumbling and running down the small hill toward his house. Stunned at the unfolding of the fight between Peterson and Johnny, Jackson had paid no attention to Henry who had slowly made his way close to the huge man. Peterson's words hung in the air as Henry dropped Johnny's greatcoat, pivoted on his feet to his right and with every ounce of strength he could muster, he brought his big left fist around and hit Jackson full in the face. Jackson responded by taking a step back and dropping the greatcoat he was holding. Henry hit him as hard as he could in his left side with his right hand. Jackson grunted and pawed at the gun on his hip. Henry jumped on him and the two hit the ground and began grappling and wrestling. Jackson hit Henry and blood poured from his nose, another blow hit him and the old open wound on Henry's face opened up and began to bleed, but Henry got his left arm free and as the two wrestled on the ground, Henry landed a hard blow to the side of Jackson's head.

Jackson tried to get to his revolver, but it had fallen out. Johnny watched for a moment, and then began to walk toward the big house, dragging his left leg.

Henry hit Jackson in the jaw with his right hand as the two, still clinging to each other rose up. The blow was solid, but Henry felt pain shoot through his hand where the snake had bitten him. Jackson landed a blow to Henry's mid-section and he felt the breath go out of him as he hugged Jackson, buying some time.

As the men came out of the bunkhouse, a shot rang out and a voice said, "Lay down or die!"

One man dove to the ground, but eight or nine others ran for the bunkhouse. Shots rang out and one man did a little dance and dropped. Another was hit in the hand, but they were close to the bunkhouse and the rest made it safely.

The five men riding in from the fields, heard the shooting over by the bunkhouse. They came into view riding hard. Pulling up in back of the big house, they began taking fire from the stables. They turned their horses and rode to the front of the house, slid off their horses, guns drawn and charged in the front door and up the stairs so they could fire from the windows.

Seeing the men and hearing the firing, Gator turned to Jameson, riding beside him and said, "I don't want to be here all day. I'm calling up the cavalry."

Jameson looked at him, confused.

"Well, it's more like thunder and lightning," said Gator smiling. "Ya'll move over yonder off the road and wait a bit."

Jameson pointed to the side of the road and Clyde and Rosalinda followed him as Gator turned his horse and waved at the men sitting on the wagon. They began to move forward and in a moment reached Gator. "Here will do. There're some fellows gonna be upstairs shooting. Just take the top floor off the place and let's see if that don't do it."

One of the men got off and began unhooking the harness from the horse and the other man climbed in the back of the wagon and threw off the tarp, revealing a huge Gatling machine gun.

As soon as the horse was moved away, the man in the wagon was ready. Firing could be heard from the back of the house. The man looked at Gator. Gator nodded and the man cranked the machine gun as the other man climbed in to help him with reloading. The sound was tremendous and the house's upper floor seemed to disappear as the heavy fifty caliber rounds chewed it up. Gator, sitting on his horse, lit a huge cigar as he watched.

Rosalinda, Clyde and Jameson watched in awe and horror at the destruction.

On the hill, Jackson brought his knee up hard, but Henry twisted just in time and then pushed away from Jackson and began hitting him with a flurry of blows. Right, left, right, left, body and face as Jackson stumbled backward, holding his arms up trying to block the blows raining on his face and body. Fury flooded Henry and he felt nothing as he pounded Jackson. Finally, exhausted and breathing hard, his legs shaky, Henry's vision cleared and he stopped, still holding his hands up as he looked at Jackson's bloody, beaten face.

"I'm fixing to kill you," said Jackson, through his bloody, broken mouth, as he reached down and pulled a knife from his boot.

He was never able to bring it up, as Henry, stepping forward with his right foot, hit him in the head with a looping right hand and stepping in with his left foot, followed it up with a left to the head. Henry was on him now and going for the knife, but there was no need. An unconscious Jackson crumbled to the ground. Soaked in blood, Henry stood over him for a moment, then picked up the knife, walked over and picked up the pistol and looked toward the house. He saw Johnny entering a door on the side of the house facing them. Then he realized shots were ringing out from the stables. He started walking toward the house, but he was moving slowly, totally spent. When the five mounted men rode into the front yard and raced into the house, Henry watched them, concerned about Johnny. He tried to increase his speed, but his legs weren't working well. He completely stopped when he heard the thundering blast of the Gatling gun.

Clyde, watching with his spyglass, almost dropped it when he saw Johnny approaching the side of the house. He looked to see if anyone was chasing him and to his amazement, saw Henry Bear standing on the side of the hill, looking up at the top of the house as the rounds from the Gatling gun destroyed it.

Turning to Jameson and Rosalinda, Clyde exclaimed, "I saw Johnny and Henry, they're alive!"

After his announcement Clyde rode his horse up to Gator and said, "One of our men has just entered the house and the other is headed toward it. Gator nodded, looked up at the house, its second floor all but gone and waved to the men manning the Gatling gun and they ceased firing.

"I think we'll move the cavalry so we can get to the bunkhouse," said Gator, but Jameson, Clyde and Rosalinda, tears streaming down her face, were all riding for the great-house, guns drawn.

The two black men who had helped Johnny dig out of the stockade, along with George, the man who had tried to escape, but was caught, made their way toward the great-house as they listened to sounds they had never heard before. They were followed by a small group of black men, some of them armed with hoes or shovels.

The shooting between Peterson's men in the bunkhouse and Gator's men at the stables was sporadic. Gator had told his men to disarm the men if they surrendered, kill them if need be, but at the least, keep them penned down and busy until told otherwise. They were doing just that and had enjoyed watching the top floor of the house flying apart as the Gatling gun's rounds tore it to pieces.

The two men that had set off the dynamite blast had disarmed the man who had been shot and fallen from his horse. They looked him over, and told him he might live, he might not and since he was out of the action left him and reported to the stables to assist in the fight there.

Seeing Henry, a black man slowly walking down the hill on the far side of the house, the group of sixteen men, led by George headed for him. When they reached him, he pointed to the top of the hill and told them they could find Jackson there.

As he turned to continue his journey to the house he said, "Slavery has been illegal for nine years. Nine years."

A half-dozen men continued up the hill, two took hold of Henry to help him walk, and another eight followed them toward the house.

Jameson entered the front door of the house first and confronted by two white men pointing pistols at him, shot them both, two rounds each. One had gotten off a shot, but it went wide. As he reloaded, Rosalinda, holding her own revolver stepped up beside him. Clyde, armed with an 1872 British Webley Bulldog he had pulled from his coat pocket, said, "I'm going down the hallway," and disappeared.

Something poked Clyde in the back and a voice said, "Drop your weapon and turn very slowly."

Clyde, bent forward and rather gently dropped his Webley Bulldog revolver on the floor, straightened up and turned to see the butler, Edwards, holding a large revolver leveled at this chest.

"You!" said Edwards, total surprise in his voice. "The Bible salesman."

"Yes, that's correct," said Clyde, "and I must say, it would have benefitted you to have purchased one and studied it."

"You are part of the gang that has attacked this household," hissed the man. "I am going to enjoy watching you die," and he raised the pistol as Clyde clutched at his chest. "What are you doing?" asked Edwards.

"Just this," said Clyde, who had stuck his hand in a vest pocket. Pulling out his hand, he thrust it toward Edward's face and shot him. The bullet entered just below his left eye and the large revolver dropped from his hand as his knees buckled and he dropped to the floor.

"What?" asked Edwards, as he tumbled onto his face.

"It's a Sharps Pepperbox. A four-shot derringer," said Clyde as he replaced the derringer in his pocket, bent and picked up his Webley Bulldog.

Johnny found Peterson in the room with the big chair, after searching through the house. Peterson was sitting in it, still holding his right hand to his neck. Only his eyes visible in his face, as blood poured from the huge gash in his forehead. Johnny walked to him, carrying the saber, his face grim. As Johnny stood, he heard noises behind him and he turned to see Henry, helped by two black men, enter the room. Other black men pushed in.

Henry stepped free of the men helping him, walked slowly over to Johnny, looked at Peterson and said, "Boss, I think we're done here. These folks got some business to see to with Lord Peterson."

Johnny looked at Henry, nodded and the two began walking out of the room. When they reached the door, Johnny turned and tossed the saber to the floor and saw the group of men surrounding Peterson. Then, he heard Rosalinda calling his name.

Rosalinda refused to let go of Johnny's arm as they made their way out of the house. Jameson and Clyde helped Henry. Once outside, Jameson found Gator, smoking a cigar and sipping from a whiskey bottle as he watched the bunkhouse.

"I reckon we're done," said Jameson. "We've got our people and they're hurt some, but they'll recover. We appreciate your help."

"Well, I ain't quite done," said Gator. "We're about to let loose a little thunder and lightening in the general direction of the bunkhouse, maybe take the roof off it. Then we're going to give the gentlemen inside an opportunity to toss out their weapons. Once that's done we're going to load the weapons in the wagon and go home. There's a large group of black folk coming his way from the direction of the sugar fields and I'd like to be gone when some of them women get here. I was looking at 'em in my glass and they do look hostile."

Jameson laughed loudly and Gator continued, "Jameson, if you ever get out to the swamps and bayous, just mention my name. You'll be welcome."

The two men shook hands.

The doctor in New Orleans was horrified at the wounds on Johnny and Henry. They told him they had been attacked by highwaymen. The doctor said Henry's facial wound looked a week old and asked why it had not been stitched closed and Henry just looked at him.

"Gentlemen, infection is our greatest enemy in both your cases. I have washed your wounds with carbolic acid, a treatment that has seen some success. Both of you are going to have large facial scars."

Standing by the wall, watching, Rosalinda said, "It's a good thing they are both married. I can't imagine a woman being attracted to either one of them, the way they look now."

Smiling, the doctor said, "Yes, they are fortunate, indeed."

The doctor said he would need to see them in a day or two, but they informed him they were traveling. He gave them both bottles of laudanum and wished them well.

Jameson and Clyde had returned the rented horses and taken everyone's gear to the ship. Clyde sent a message via telegram, to the Menger, with instructions for it to be taken quickly to the Black homestead. Rosalinda didn't want her parents to worry a second longer than was necessary. A large buggy, with a driver, engaged by Clyde, was waiting outside the doctor's office. The group made the ship with an hour to spare.

Standing by the rail, Rosalinda said, "Johnny Black, you are never leaving the state again without me."

Smiling, Johnny asked, "Was you just funning when you told the doctor no woman would be attracted to me and Henry now?"

Smiling herself, Rosalinda said, "Maybe."

EPILOGUE

Gator and his men didn't fire the Gatling gun again. After a warning, the men in the bunkhouse threw all of their weapons outside. Within minutes, Gator's men had the guns and a dozen knives loaded in the wagon and were headed home.

They had rounded a curve in the road and were out of sight, when a large group of angry folks from the cabins swarmed the bunkhouse and great-house.

Three months after Johnny and Henry's escape, the parish sheriff, not having heard from Lord Peterson in a while, rode out to the Peterson Sugar Plantation and Mill. He was shocked to see the upper portion of the great-house missing and decided it had been destroyed by a tornado. An even greater shock occurred when the sheriff realized the place was abandoned. There wasn't a human, animal, or wagon to be found.

Finding the front door unbolted, he entered and found the heavy rains in the last few months had taken a toll on the interior. It was odd, he thought, that Lord Peterson had not taken any of the large paintings or furniture with him. Lord Peterson had always been friendly to him and the sheriff couldn't understand why the man hadn't contacted him. There had been rumors the man was holding the blacks working on his plantation as slaves, but the sheriff had brought some army officers out some time back and they determined all was well.

There were no bodies and no other sign of a crime, so the sheriff shrugged, and taking notice of dark clouds building in the north, made haste for home.

Caleb made it to Missouri in record time. He and Mollie were married a month later. While on their honeymoon, Mollie told Caleb she was rich and she, her mother and uncle owned the bank that had belonged to her father.

"I don't care if you are rich, I still love you," announced Caleb.

The local sheriff rode out one day to tell Mollie an outlaw gang had tried to rob a bank in San Antonio, but the bank had been tipped off and all the men were captured. Mollie told her mother and they cried.

Mollie and Caleb bought a ranch with a large house on it and four months later, Mollie told Caleb he was going to be a father. That evening, after supper, sitting outside, smoking, Caleb thought about B.R. and how he missed him, but, he realized, he had found his place in this world and he was happy; very happy.

B.R. asked Topsannah why his washing dishes had opened her heart to him. She replied, "I am a widow and many men come around, but they don't want to marry me." She smiled. "When you worked so hard and I wasn't even there, I knew you were serious about me."

One day, not long after Caleb left, Mr. Christie called Billy Ray into his office.

"Come in B.R." said Christie. "How you doing these days?"

"I'm good Mr. Christie. Real good. Thinking to ask a girl to marry me."

"You found one to ask yet?"

"Huh? Oh, yes, I mean yes sir, I've found one."

"You know, cowboys are as bad as old women when it comes to one of their own. I knew about you and Topsannah nearly before you did. I met the young lady at the barn dance. She's a looker if you don't mind me saying."

Billy Ray was stunned to hear Mr. Christie say Topsannah's name.

"Now I want you to understand something. You're doing a right fine job here by all accounts."

Billy Ray's stomach fell. Mr. Christie was letting him go.

"Let me get to it. You remember Johnny Black?"

B.R. had ridden on a cattle drive financed and put together by Mr. Christie, with Johnny Black as trail boss.

"I don't reckon I'll ever forget Boss Black," replied B.R.

"Well, I run across him in town the other day and we visited a little and he's looking for a top-notch beeve and horse man to head up that part of his operation. He's doing some farming and has a good man heading that up. Against my better judgement, cause it's not in my best interest, I told him you had come along and would likely fit that bill; if a man weren't too awful particular, but you was likely going to be marrying soon, that is, if Topsannah don't come to her senses."

B.R. heard Mr. Christie, but his voice seemed far away. Was something good happening here, he wondered?

"Any no how, Johnny is interested in talking to you and if you're interested, he's expecting you at his place daybreak in the morning. I've told the foreman you're to have the day off if you are a mind to see Black."

B.R. went to work for Johnny Black, building a small house not far from Henry Bear's. He took over the beeve and horse operation, while Henry continued to head up the expanding farming and produce side.

Billy Ray's friend, Jace and his wife, Ruth, were living north of the Black spread, raising sheep and cattle up on the Edwards Plateau. When B.R. rode in with Topsannah by his side, to invite Jace and Ruth to his wedding, a tearful, but happy reunion took place. Jace had ridden with B.R. on the trail drive led by Johnny; it was where he had met Ruth, and he was happy to catch up on news regarding Johnny and his family.

In the Spring of 1875, Topsannah and Billy Ray wed at the Black ranch. Topsannah quickly found herself fast friends with Rosalinda and Venus. The three women were busy and happy, making soap, putting up vegetables, gardening, quilting and sewing. Six months after their wedding, Topsannah told the girls she was with child. Rosalinda was thrilled, not least because little Lucrecia would soon have a playmate. That afternoon, Topsannah told B.R..

After an evening of celebration, sitting outside by himself, it occurred to him that he was likely the most blessed man on earth. He and Caleb write each other.

When they reached San Antonio, Clyde presented his bill to Johnny who expressed outrage at the total sum as he laughed. The two shook hands and Clyde caught the stagecoach to Austin.

After they stepped off the stagecoach in San Antonio, Johnny and Jameson shook hands. "Jameson," said Johnny, "I never, ever would have thought our trip to Waelder in the rain would turn into such an adventure."

"Nor I," said Jameson.

Johnny tried to pay him, but he wouldn't accept it. However, a fine riding horse, fitted with a new saddle and bridle, was tied to a tree outside his little cabin one day. A note and bill of sale in Jameson's name was pinned to the saddle blanket. The note read: *My name is Sugar.* Jameson visits the Black homestead from time to time. He's very happy. He met a good woman and he's enjoying sharing his life with her.

Henry Bear healed up from the snake bite, the beating and the fight with Jackson. Venus thinks the scar on his face adds character to it. While he was gone, Venus took to visiting Henry's two cats who lived in the barn and when Henry returned, to his surprise he found that although the cats still visited the barn, they had taken up residence in the Bear home. Henry Bear and Venus can often be seen picnicking on Sundays, or walking in the evenings, arm in arm.

On the trip home from New Orleans, Jameson and Bear took to calling Rosalinda and Johnny, the lovebirds, when they weren't around. The two were inseparable and seeing them look at each other made both men shake their heads.

"You'd think they just met," said Jameson.

"That's a fact. Johnny got that dazed look young men get when they've fallen hard," said Bear and both men laughed.

Arriving home, Rosalinda stepped down from the buggy and helped Johnny. His wounded leg was stiff and painful. Standing by the buggy, Rosalinda suddenly let out a yell. Laughing, she took off running. Startled, Johnny turned his head to see a pack of dogs bearing down on him at a dead run. Given his bad leg, Johnny had the presence of mind to sit down, but he just made it as Flop hit him in the chest, knocking him onto his back and within seconds, three dogs were on top of Johnny, licking him.

"Flop, Princesa, Perro," he managed to blurt out as he hugged and rubbed the dogs.

Johnny had just made it to his feet when a huge, dark horse thundered into the yard, coming to a stop not far from Johnny, then walking forward. "Loco!" exclaimed Johnny, as the big horse lowered its head and pushed it into Johnny's chest. Johnny grabbed it and pressed his own to it.

Visiting the barn, Johnny was thrilled to find eighteen new foals. As he stood in the corral, he was nudged in the back and turning, found himself face to face with a horse he didn't recognize. The horse bobbed his head and neighed. Suddenly Johnny realized this fine-looking animal was the starving horse he had bought just before Thanksgiving.

That evening, Lucrecia, who had been allowed to stay up late to play with her father, finally fell asleep and was placed in her bed. Johnny and Rosalinda retired to the porch, and sat, sipping coffee, as they did most evenings. They didn't speak tonight. There was no need.

The end.

Made in the USA
Columbia, SC
03 July 2024